Del

Macklins of Whiskey Bend, Book Two
Contemporary Western Romance

SHIRLEEN DAVIES

Books Series by Shirleen Davies

<u>Historical Western Romances</u>

Redemption Mountain
MacLarens of Fire Mountain Historical
MacLarens of Boundary Mountain

<u>Romantic Suspense</u>

Eternal Brethren Military Romantic Suspense
Peregrine Bay Romantic Suspense

<u>Contemporary Western Romance</u>

MacLarens of Fire Mountain Contemporary
Macklins of Whiskey Bend

The best way to stay in touch is to subscribe to my newsletter. Go to my Website *www.shirleendavies.com* and fill in your email and name in the Join My Newsletter boxes. That's it!

Description

__Two fractured hearts.__
__One chance to correct the mistakes from their__
__past.__

Delaware "Del" Macklin has made a lot of choices in his life. Becoming a deputy, then sheriff instead of working full-time at the family ranch was a difficult decision...but it had been his to make. The one choice that mattered most was taken from him when the girl he'd fallen for left Whiskey Bend, creating a hole in his life and his heart.

Amy Peterson is on a mission, one leading her back to Whiskey Bend after years away. Certain her mother's death wasn't an accident, she refuses to allow threats or intimidation to stop her search for the truth. Encountering Del Macklin, the boy she fell for in school, could either be an answer to her prayers or a distraction she can't afford.

Finding Amy after all these years is a welcome surprise. Discovering the reason she's in town, and the danger surrounding her, isn't. As sheriff, he's required to follow the law, even if it means sending her to jail. As a man, his protective instincts roar to life, urging him to guard her in every way possible.

As the mystery of her mother's death unfolds, feelings they'd both ignored when younger come thundering back, complicating a situation already thick with emotion.

Can Amy find the courage to risk her heart for another chance?

Will Del ignore the warnings and seize the choice taken from him years before?

Del, book two in the Macklins of Whiskey Bend Contemporary Western Romance series, is a stand-alone, full-length novel with an HEA and no cliffhanger.

Del

Prologue

Whiskey Bend, Montana

Delaware "Del" Macklin tried to focus on the speakers, not the sense of loss he felt during the memorial service for Mike Weiker. He still hadn't come to terms with his high school science teacher, one of the best men he'd ever known, being gone.

As sheriff, he tried to attend services for as many locals as he could, believing it a duty and an honor. His appearance today had nothing to do with his position in the community and everything to do with the man who'd left this world much too soon.

Del knew the service affected his two brothers as much as him. Thorn, the oldest, stood in his U.S. Army Special Forces uniform, while the youngest, Daniel "Boone" Macklin, wore his best jeans, polished boots, and cowboy hat. They, along with so many others, had a special relationship with Weiker.

"Beer?" Thorn clasped his shoulder, Boone standing on his other side.

Blinking a couple times, Del shook his head, realizing he'd missed the last speaker and the end of the service. Letting out a breath, he nodded. "Sure. Kull's place?"

"Yeah. You can ride over with me. Boone is meeting Shane Taggart and Jerry Cooper at Evie's Diner. They'll probably come to Kull's afterward."

Thorn led the way to his truck, sending and receiving thoughtful nods from those still milling around. "Helluva thing."

Del glanced at him, lifting a brow. "What?"

"The number of people Weiker touched during his life. I doubt there will ever be anyone else quite like him. It makes me feel bad for the kids in Whiskey Bend."

Shoving his hands into his pockets, Del followed behind, not quite ready to let the past go, knowing he had no choice. After high school, he'd meet up with Weiker during college breaks, then a few times for coffee after he became a deputy. Since becoming sheriff, Del's free time had been cut to nothing, giving them few chances to catch up. He found himself wishing for one more day with the man. One more round of local craft beer and pool at Kull's bar, Wicked Waters, while he and Weiker laughed about anything and everything.

Reaching for the back passenger door of Thorn's truck, Del's hand stilled, his chest tightening. A lone figure stood with her arms clasped around her waist, face ashen, staring at the dispersing crowd. So lost in her own thoughts, she didn't notice him.

His mind flashed back to high school and a lithe, beautiful girl with long blonde hair and bright green eyes. Her quick, easy smile had drawn him to her the first day they'd shared a table during Weiker's science class. Even then, she'd been as elusive as a butterfly, drifting in and out of Del's life, until the summer after their junior year when her family moved away, leaving a void in his life he'd never been able to fill.

He shot a look at his brothers. "Hold up a minute. There's someone I want to say hello to." When he turned back, she was gone.

"Who?" Thorn asked, looking around.

"She was right over there a few seconds ago." Del shifted, scanning the area for any trace of her.

"Who, Del?" Thorn pressed, wondering if his brother had conjured up an illusion.

A frustrated breath escaped as he shook his head. "A girl I knew in high school. But I must have been wrong." Climbing into the truck, he glanced over his shoulder as Thorn pulled away.

His heart pounded. He was certain he'd seen her. The same as in high school, she'd disappeared as fast as a leaf in a strong wind.

Del couldn't help but wonder at her return and if she'd come to stay. After all this time, maybe he'd have another chance with the girl who'd stolen his heart all those years ago.

Chapter One

A few months later...

"Is my order ready, Evie?" Del stood at the counter, digging into his wallet to pull out some bills as he glanced around at the crowd. He waved at Agua and Blake Stone, then saw Shane and Mason Taggart at a nearby table.

Lifting his chin in acknowledgment, he started to make his way toward them before Evie called to him. "Here you go, Sheriff. The same as always...ham and cheese on sourdough with fries. You know, Del, it wouldn't hurt you to change it up once in a while. The menu is loaded with a lot of other great food. You've got five sandwiches in there. Ask one of your deputies for a bite of theirs."

Chuckling, he handed her the money, sliding the wallet back into his pocket. He'd known Evie Denton most of his life. A couple years older than him, she and her husband owned Evie's Diner, a popular breakfast and lunch spot, and a favorite of the law enforcement crowd.

"Will you get off my back if I try something else tomorrow?"

Her eyes lit up, as if he'd just given her a thirty dollar tip. "Can't promise you that, but I'll make you something extra special. I mean, what do you have to lose?"

His face scrunched up. "My appetite?"

"Very funny. Anything new happening around town?"

Grinning, he picked up the bag. "I come in here to learn the latest news, Evie, not spread it. Thanks." Heading to the door, he turned back. "Hey, do you remember Amy Peterson from high school?"

"Hmmm...Amy Peterson." Her brows drew together before her features stilled. "Long blonde hair and gorgeous eyes? I think she was your age."

"That's her. Did you ever hear what happened to her?"

"I didn't keep up much after graduation." She thought a moment. "Wait. I do remember her dad getting arrested and sent off to prison." Evie didn't notice Del's jaw drop or eyes widen. "I think that's why her mom decided to move."

"Prison?"

"Yeah. Her dad, Pete Peterson, was high in the ranks of a motorcycle gang. I remember my husband talking about it. Of course, we weren't married then. Peterson got caught up in some arms trafficking sting operation by the Feds. I'm sure you can go online and get the dirty details. Why are you asking?"

He shrugged, although he couldn't wait to get out of the diner and on a computer. "No reason, other than I thought I saw her at Mike Weiker's memorial service. Haven't seen her since."

"It's doubtful you will. From the little I know, they hightailed it out of here after the trial." Evie leaned over the counter. "She was a sweet girl. Kind of quiet, but real nice. You know what I mean?"

Del thought back on their conversations during science and at lunch...when he could convince her to sit with him. Sweet and nice described her, as did pretty, funny, and shy. He should've asked more about her, found out why she dodged most of his questions and turned down his invitations to a movie or dinner.

"Yeah, I know what you mean. Guess I'd better head back and feed my deputies." He waved at Shane and Mason. "I'll catch up with you two later."

The county building, home to the sheriff's office, stood a few blocks away. Instead of heading back, he decided to take a small detour, see if his brother, Thorn, might be working. He and two buddies from high school owned Scorpion Custom Motorcycles, making a name for themselves fabricating custom bikes.

Thorn knelt down beside a bike in the front parking area, checking it out, while a young man in leathers and work boots stood next to him.

"We can fix this, but it won't be ready until tomorrow afternoon." Thorn stood, taking one more look at the bike.

"That's fine. Do I need to sign anything?"

"I'll have Tony prepare a work order with the details and your contact information. Someone will call when it's ready. Follow me inside and we'll get it started."

"Thanks, man. I appreciate it."

"Hey, Thorn."

Turning, he grinned, seeing his brother carrying a large sack. "Del. What brings you over here?"

He held up the bag. "Lunch for my people."

"I thought you had clerks for that."

"Clerks? Not on my budget. The deputies are the clerks and I'm the gofer half the time. Do you have a minute?" Del shifted the sack to the other hand.

"Give me a minute to talk to Tony and get this customer's order going."

Following Thorn inside, a slight grin crossed Del's face when he saw the finished bikes in the showroom. A few weeks before, there'd been a series of arson fires, threatening the new operation. All seemed to be going smoothly now.

Thorn walked up to him. "Okay. What's up?"

"Have you ever heard of a guy named Pete Peterson?"

"Hell yeah. Most everyone has heard of him. At least those who ride. At the time, you were probably too focused on getting into college to pay any attention." Thorn glanced around, nodding for them to move outside. "Why are you asking?"

"First, tell me what you know."

Pinching the bridge of his nose, Thorn's eyes narrowed. "You can find all this online, but Pete's the president of the Savage Wolves Motorcycle Club. In reality, it's a gang. From what I've heard, they're involved in all sorts of stuff."

"Like?"

"Guns, drugs, maybe human trafficking. Bad stuff, Del. He went to prison after I graduated from high school, but he's back out, running the club." Thorn scrubbed a hand down his face, his lips drawing into a thin line. "He came in here a few weeks ago. Asked about a custom bike, although I don't know why. The Wolves have their own shop east of Missoula."

"Are you doing the work?"

"I haven't heard back. What's all this about, Del?" Thorn crossed his arms, leaning against the outside wall.

"His name came up when I asked Evie about a classmate of mine from high school. Turns out she's Peterson's daughter."

Thorn nodded, his lips quirking up at the corners. "Ah, the elusive Amy Peterson."

For the second time in less than thirty minutes, Del's jaw dropped.

"Hey, don't look so surprised. You were completely locked into her during your sophomore and junior years." Thorn laughed at Del's stunned expression. "Don't tell me you thought I didn't know. I'm your older brother. I knew a lot about what was going on with you in high school."

Sucking in a breath, Del let it out in a slow whoosh. "We never dated. I never saw her outside of school."

"Yeah, but you wanted to. I figured she was why you didn't go out much." Thorn's face sobered as he clasped his brother on the shoulder. "Is she the girl you thought you saw at Weiker's service?"

"Oh, I saw her. She rocketed out of there when she spotted me. That's my theory anyway."

"Can't blame her. You're the sheriff. Her dad's an ex-con, and there's a good chance he'll be a *future* con. You're probably the last person she wants to see."

Del nodded, not liking the fact he agreed with Thorn. "It doesn't matter. I haven't seen her since. I'm pretty certain she came in for the service and left." Shifting the sack once more, he headed toward the street, then turned back. "Let me know if you hear anything more from Peterson."

"You got it."

Del's sandwich lay untouched next to his computer. Other than a few short interruptions, he'd been researching Savage Wolves Motorcycle Club and Pete Peterson for over an hour, finding no shortage of information. As far as he could tell, Peterson had spent less than two years in prison before returning to the Wolves. Since then, there were a few arrests of other club members, but nothing more on Pete.

"Interesting guy."

Del glanced over his shoulder to see one of his senior deputies looking at the screen. "You know about him, Joe?"

"Who doesn't?"

Del winced, not answering. "Tell me what you know." He swiveled to face him, pointing to another chair.

Joe Nolen had been a deputy in Whiskey Bend since before the Macklin boys were in middle school. Of average height with thinning brown hair, he sported a slight paunch, which he'd proudly pat, saying it was the right of passage for men in their forties.

Lowering himself into the chair, he bent forward, resting his hands on his thighs. "What do you want to know?"

"I can't find much in the last few years on him or the club. The record is sparse, except for a few arrests resulting in little time. Where are they located?"

"Used to be they had a clubhouse quite a ways outside of Missoula. That changed when Pete went to prison." Leaning back in his chair, he rubbed his chin. "You were probably in high school at the time. Anyway, he got out about two years later and moved the club to White Basin, east of Helena. I've been fishing out that way and it's not much more than a dot on the map. A few thousand people. The Wolves have chapters in Bozeman and Billings, but the real business is controlled out of White Basin."

"Are they still trading in the same stuff as when Pete was convicted?"

Resting his right ankle over his left thigh, Joe crossed his arms. "His arrest was about illegal firearms, and yeah, they're still into that. At least that's what our counterparts in that area of Montana are saying. The Wolves have been involved in extortion, prostitution, drug trafficking, contract murder. You name it, they've probably done it.

My understanding is most of their money comes from their meth business.”

“Feds still after them?”

Joe barked out a laugh. “The Feds are *always* after the outlaw gangs. Why are you asking all these questions? Have you seen them around Whiskey Bend?”

Del thought about asking Joe what he knew about Peterson’s family, deciding to find answers himself. His interest in Amy showing up at the memorial service needed to stay quiet.

“Heard the name and got curious. Nothing more.” Closing his laptop, Del picked up his sandwich. “Thanks, Joe. I appreciate the information.”

“You know, if you really want the latest on Pete and his club, you ought to talk to Kull.”

Del choked on the bite he’d just taken, forcing the food down his throat. “Kull Kacey?”

Walking away, Joe looked over his shoulder. “You know anyone else named Kull?”

Grabbing a bottle of water, he took a long swallow, deciding how to approach the man who’d been a friend to Del and his brothers since high school. He, Thorn, and Boone had always gotten along better with Kull than they had with their own father—may he rest in peace.

Kull had supported them, been an open ear when their father made life miserable on the ranch. He’d sold Thorn the property where Scorpion Custom Motorcycles now operated, letting his brother use the contacts Kull had made customizing individual bikes for over twenty years.

The man still called all of them *son*, giving each of them a hug when they visited Wicked Waters for drinks.

Del mentally slapped himself on the forehead for not thinking of Kull sooner. A Vietnam veteran, most considered him an old-timer with a lot of history tucked under the baseball cap he favored. You wanted to know about skeletons in someone's closet, you went to Kull.

He just needed to figure out the right way to approach him, consider his questions carefully before talking to him. The last thing Del needed was for word to get out he'd been asking questions about the club, its members, and their families. And he needed to shield Amy. No matter who her father was or what he'd done, Del didn't want anything to blow back on her. If anyone knew about the sins of their fathers, it was the Macklin boys.

"Bobby?" Del grabbed the well-worn cowboy hat he favored, tossed his sandwich wrapping in the trash, then picked up his keys.

"Yeah, boss." The twenty-something deputy looked twelve, but was one of his best men.

"I'm taking off for a bit. Everyone's got their assignments, but call me if anything comes up."

"Sure, Sheriff." Bobby turned back to his desk, then jumped up at what sounded like an explosion. "Holy..."

Del ran to the front window, Bobby right behind him, to see black smoke rising a block or two behind Thorn's shop.

"Change in plans." Del turned. "I'm heading over to find out what just happened." Dashing outside, he jumped into his county-issued truck. He could have walked—might have even been faster—but he wanted to use the lights and siren to get up close before those too curious to stay away clogged the roads.

Winding through the streets, he pulled to within a hundred yards of what had been a small clapboard house a couple blocks from the town's main street. Dark smoke poured out of the windows, onlookers pushing to get closer than they should.

Jumping out of his truck, Del saw the fire engine turn onto the street, pulling to a stop in front of the burning structure. On instinct, he instructed the bystanders to move to the other side of the street and down the block as two patrol cars pulled up, followed by an unmarked car.

Del walked toward the plainclothesman who got out, extending his hand. "Detective Zoeller."

"You got here fast, Sheriff." Rick Zoeller grasped the offered hand.

"I was headed out anyway. The explosion had me moving faster."

Rick grinned, then sobered. "Wonder what caused it."

"Leak in a gas line, burning cigarette, unattended candle. Who knows? I suppose they'll be calling in that investigator from Missoula."

Nodding, Rick pulled out a notepad and pen. "Jillian Somerville. Either her or one of the others."

Turning, they watched as the firefighters worked to control the blaze before it spread to neighboring houses. Del was just about to shift back toward Rick when he spotted someone running behind the houses next to the burning building.

"Excuse me."

Del took off at a run, not hearing Rick call his name. Slipping between the houses, he saw a slim figure, wearing slacks and a hoodie, dart down the alley, skirting trash cans and cars.

"Stop!" Del shouted, not surprised when the figure skidded around a corner. Determined to catch the person, he picked up speed. He hadn't run this hard in years, his breath already becoming labored.

Stopping where the alley met a side street, he placed fisted hands on his hips, sucking in air as he looked around. He was about to turn back when he caught sight of the figure again, taking a turn. Del knew exactly which way to go next.

Running in the opposite direction, he made his way through two narrow passageways between buildings before taking a turn onto a narrow road. A smile crossed his face at the sound of footfalls coming toward him. Easing back into a doorway, he waited.

Less than a minute later, he heard the steps slow to a walk, the sound of deep breathing only a few yards away. Drawing his gun, he inched from the doorway, pointing it at the suspect's back.

"Don't move."

The person took a tentative step away, not turning to look at him.

"I said, do...not...move. Get your hands where I can see them and turn around."

Slowly, the arms came up as the person shifted, keeping their face lowered. The hoodie made it hard for him to get a good look.

Walking forward, Del made a visual sweep of the clothing, not seeing anything to indicate the person had a weapon. Still, you could never be sure. He'd need to do a protective search. He continued to train his gun on the person's chest.

"Remove the hood."

Shaky hands took hold of the fabric, pushing it back, raising an unsteady gaze to meet Del's.

His breath caught, chest tightening at the sight of long blonde hair and brilliant green eyes. "Amy? What the hell..."

Chapter Two

"Hello, Del." A grim smile appeared on Amy's face. Taking a slow step forward, she started to lower her arms.

"Keep them up."

She jerked to a stop, her lips parting as if she wanted to say more. Moving her arms higher, Amy looked away as he took a step closer.

"Hold your arms out to your sides."

Complying with Del's order, she bit her lip, feeling his hand make a quick search of her outer clothing before he stepped away. Amy hadn't realized she'd been holding her breath until he lowered his gun.

"You can put your arms down."

Nodding, she did as he said, still not meeting his gaze. When he didn't say more, she wrapped her arms around her waist, drawing in an unsteady breath.

"Look at me, Amy."

Shaking her head, she closed her eyes, fear and humiliation washing over her. The last person Amy wanted to run into was Del Macklin, the boy who'd meant so much to her at a time when her life had been falling apart. A boy who never knew how much she cared about him.

"Amy, you need to look at me. Please."

The sound of an approaching siren had her scooting a few feet away. As the sound came closer, she shot a panicked look at Del, seeing his brows furrow. Before he knew what had happened, she shot past him, running toward a low fence at the end of the street.

Mumbling a curse, he started running, almost reaching her before she leapt into the air and hurled herself over the fence, landing on her feet. Not bothering to look behind her, Amy took off toward an apartment complex fifty yards away, disappearing between two buildings.

Del didn't even try to hurdle the fence, knowing his already damaged knees would suffer the consequences. Running along the fence line, he pushed through a gate, continuing toward the complex of four buildings, each two stories high. At this time in the afternoon, kids played in the wide parking area, adults returned from work or headed out, and teenagers hung out, leaning against cars in dire need of new paint. A quick count told Del there had to be twenty people outside.

"Okay, everyone. Listen up. Anyone see a woman run through here?"

"What kind of woman?"

Del shot a look at the teenage boy. "The female kind. Long blonde hair, wearing jeans and a hoodie."

"Sorry, Sheriff. Haven't seen that kind of woman." The kid laughed as he turned toward his buddies.

Del shook his head in frustration. "Anyone else see anybody matching the description?"

An older woman walked up to him. For an instant, Del thought he'd caught a break.

"Did you see her, ma'am?"

"Nope, didn't see anybody. But my television got stolen last night." She pointed to the group of teenage boys. "One of them took it."

Settling his hands on his hips, he sighed. "Did you report it stolen, ma'am?"

"Well, that's what I'm doing now."

He blew out a relieved breath when a police car stopped at the curb, a female officer climbing out. Walking up to him, a smile spread across her face.

"Trouble, Del?"

"Nothing I can't handle, Lucy. But if you're offering to help..."

She didn't have a chance to reply before the woman walked up to her. "My television is gone again, Lucy."

Forcing back a grin, Lucy walked up to the woman, placing a hand on her shoulder. "Mrs. Kline, why don't you show me the last place you remember seeing it." Looking over her shoulder, she shot an amused glance at Del, letting him know she'd take care of it.

Crossing his arms, he took a slow turn of the parking lot, looking at each building, knowing he wouldn't see her. Amy had disappeared...again.

"Heard you saw your ghost, Del." Daniel "Boone" Macklin, his younger brother, strolled into Del's house two nights later, not bothering to stop before heading to the kitchen for a beer.

It was the same every Wednesday night. Had been for months. Boone came to town after a full day on the ranch, drank a couple beers out of Del's refrigerator, talked for about an hour, then left to visit some unnamed female friend. His brothers had no idea of the identity of the woman, figuring Boone would bring her around if it ever got serious. He never had.

"Heard you caught her, she batted those gorgeous green eyes at you, then took off, leaving you with your tongue hanging out."

Del tossed down the TV remote and stood, going to the kitchen to grab his own beer. "The least you could do is bring over a six-pack every once in a while."

Boone held up the bottle of craft beer. "Hey, I don't have the budget for the upscale stuff you drink." Taking another swallow, he sat down in Del's favorite leather chair. "At least I have one brother with good taste."

Del swatted the back of Boone's head, encouraging him to vacate the chair before Del forced him to move. Taking Boone's place, he pushed the button to recline the back.

"Talk to Thorn about whiskey sometime. The man is a connoisseur."

"I've never seen him so, well...happy. It's almost nauseating."

Del raised a brow. "You'd be happy, too, if you married a woman like Grace."

"As far as I can tell, he got the last good woman in Whiskey Bend. Pretty soon, we're going to have to start looking in Missoula."

Shaking his head, Del took another sip of beer. "Yeah. Tell me what you find." Leaning forward, he snagged the remote, flipping through several channels.

"Back to the gossip. Was the woman who got away really your long-lost Amy Peterson?"

Del tossed the remote at him. "You find something, and she is definitely *not* my anything."

Settling on a true crime show, Boone rested his feet on the coffee table, earning a glare from his brother. "But it was Amy, right?"

Rubbing his brow with a finger, Del nodded. "Yeah, it was Amy."

"So what was the deal? Do you think she started the fire?"

Del didn't think so. Still... "Who knows? Jillian Somerville determined it was arson, Amy was running from the scene, and we have no other suspects. Rick Zoeller is investigating."

"Good ol' Rick. How's he doing?" Boone changed the channel to some reality show.

Zoeller had been a touchy subject when Grace dated him for a while before getting back together with Thorn. No one except Grace seemed to know the detective's story, and she wasn't talking.

"He's a good man. Dedicated, thorough. Wish we had more like him. Whatever he went through before is his business. As long as he does his job, I'm okay with him."

"And sweet Officer Lucy. You *okay* with her, too?"

Del stood, flipping him off as he took his empty bottle into the kitchen.

"Not talking, huh?" Boone followed his brother.

Del turned, leaning close to Boone's face. "Lucy is off limits. She's a good lady who deserves a break after all she went through with her deadbeat husband."

A few years earlier, Del had helped her when she left the man, taking their baby son with her. The police chief had given her a couple months off with partial pay, but things had been tight. The Macklin brothers offered her one of the houses they owned in town, rent free, until she got herself back together. She still lived there, paying full rent.

After the divorce, Lucy and Del fell into a short fling, but it never went anywhere. They'd both been glad it ended with them staying friends.

Holding up his hands, Boone backed off. "I didn't mean anything by it. She *is* a good woman, and I admire what she's done." Pulling out his phone, he read something, then tapped a reply. "I'd better get going. Thanks for the beer."

Del followed him to the door, waiting until Boone had stepped outside. "Are Thorn and I ever going to meet your mystery woman?"

Turning, Boone shoved his hands into his pockets. "No."

Del had never seen his brother so tight-lipped about a woman. "Seems it's been going on a while."

Tipping his head back, Boone glanced up at the clear sky. "She's a friend. And before you ask, she's in complete agreement. No harm, no foul, brother." Something flickered across Boone's face, then vanished just as quickly. "You still meeting Thorn and me at the ranch Saturday?"

"I'll be there bright and early, so have coffee ready. From what you said needs doing, I figure we'll be working all day."

Boone nodded. "There's no shortage of work on a ranch." Turning, he held up his hand. "See you Saturday."

Del watched him climb into the old, battered pickup that had been at the ranch for years. Thorn tried to encourage him to get a new one, but Boone said it suited him fine. Besides, it had been their mother's favorite mode of transportation before she and their father died in a plane crash.

Before pulling away, Boone gave one last wave, his face showing no indication of anything going on. Del knew differently. Something was definitely going on in his brother's life, and he meant to find out what.

Going back inside, Del fell into his chair. Glancing at the table, his eyes landed on the yearbook from his junior year in high school, glad Boone hadn't noticed it. Picking it up, he flipped through the pages until he found what he wanted—Amy Peterson's picture. He'd been looking at it off and on since seeing her at the memorial service. Since the fire, he'd stared at her face for hours, wondering what had happened and why she fled. He hadn't missed the panic in her eyes, the coiled tension in the way she stood. If it had been anyone else, Del would've prepared himself for the person to flee. He hadn't expected it of Amy.

Flipping through a few more pages, he stopped on one showing a collage of different students. His favorite included a shot of him and Amy at lunch, their heads together. No matter how many women he dated, or how much he tried to purge Amy from his thoughts, he'd never quite been able to do so. It seemed strange. They'd been friends, had never dated, yet he'd always felt she was *the one*. Then, just after their junior year, she and her mother had disappeared.

Del had never spoken about Amy to Thorn, and would have never considered mentioning her to Boone. Thorn would've respected Del's privacy, kept the information to himself. His younger brother wouldn't have been so inclined.

Setting the yearbook aside, Del stood, walking to the table where he'd left his laptop. Amy's appearance had escalated his need to discover whatever he could about her and the Peterson family. He searched for almost an hour, finding nothing new.

Glancing over his shoulder, Del spotted a photograph of him and Mike Weiker taken a few years before. His throat thickened, an ache pulsing in his chest. He missed the man. His friend's death forced Del to accept the sad fact that sometimes you didn't know how much a person meant to you until they were gone. Another fact was harder to accept. Del missed Weiker more than he missed his own father.

Del's gaze moved to another picture. This one of his family before their parents died in the plane crash. He and his brothers were grown. Dressed in his army fatigues, Thorn stood between Del and Boone. Their parents sat in front of them. He'd never noticed it before, but studying the picture tonight, he realized how all their smiles seemed forced, as if no one wanted to be there.

Reaching behind him, he grabbed the frame, his gaze moving from one person to the next. He'd thought perhaps his eyes were tired from too much time researching the Petersons. Blowing out a weary breath, Del felt a stab of remorse at how distant his family had become in the years just before his parents died. Afterward, he and Boone made it a point to have dinner together at least twice a week, Del working the ranch whenever possible. When Thorn left the military, he fell right into their schedule, making time for dinner and helping to keep the ranch going.

Del guessed if the three had a new picture taken today, the faces staring back at him would be much different.

Setting the frame back on the shelf, he returned his attention to the screen. Typing in a different string of search words, his brows rose when a new article appeared.

Scanning it, he checked the time, then picked up the phone.

"Sheriff McNabb, it's Del Macklin."

"It's been a long time, Del. What can I do for you?"

"I'm headed your way tomorrow. Do you have time to meet with me?"

"Let me check the schedule. Like you, I have little control over it. Let's see. How about ten o'clock?"

"I'll be there."

"Can you tell me what this is about?"

Del thought a moment before responding. "Pete Peterson."

McNabb didn't answer for a long moment, then let out a low curse. "I got a file cabinet on the man. Be prepared to dig if I don't have a ready answer for you."

"Understood, Sheriff. See you in the morning." Del hung up, setting the phone down as he read the article one more time.

The story was several years old, written by a reporter for a small newspaper outside Missoula. A link led him to a previous article by the same reporter written a few weeks earlier. At the end of that article, there was another link, taking him to the first story in the series. It focused on Peter Peterson, his wife, and daughter, who the reporter cited as Amelia.

Leaning back in his chair, Del rubbed the back of his neck, remembering the day he and Amy had talked about their families. She'd asked him what Del was short for. He'd made her swear never to mention it to anyone. He could still recall her laughter when he'd told her his mother named him after the state where she grew up. Delaware.

When he'd asked her if Amy was short for another name, she'd raised her chin, looking him square in the eyes, and said Amelia. She'd been named after her grandmother, her mother's mother, who'd died just after Amy's sixth birthday. Del nodded, telling her it was a beautiful name. He still felt the same.

Expelling a slow breath, he touched the command to print. Collecting all three articles, he folded them, setting them next to his phone. Tomorrow, he'd continue his search for Amy. This time, he'd find her.

Chapter Three

The sun had been up for an hour when Del climbed into his SUV and headed toward the neighboring county. He took a sip of the coffee he'd purchased on his way out of town, wincing at the bitter taste. Setting it in the cup holder, he thought of what he'd learned the last few days.

On his deputy's advice, Del spoke with Kull Kacey the evening after the fire. Over a couple beers, Kull had provided him with more information than he'd been able to glean through formal channels and informal searches.

Kull had known Pete for years, long before the Macklin boys had found him a good sounding board when life on the ranch beat them down. He and Pete had become close over their love of motorcycles and the freedom it offered. Savage Wolves MC had been in its infancy, Pete earning the rank of vice president.

Married with a daughter, Kull remembered him as committed to the club first, his family second. Pete had never availed himself of the women who hung around the club...until one fateful day. The betrayal had devastated his wife, leading her to move to Whiskey Bend with their daughter. As far as Kull knew, Vivian never filed for divorce.

According to Kull, Vivian had been visited by federal agents several times before Pete's arrest and conviction. The rumors he'd heard indicated she'd never offered any information on Pete or the club. Within weeks of his conviction, she and Amy left town. Some said she moved to Idaho, others Wyoming, and a few thought she'd hightailed it back east.

Kull told Del he knew for a fact they'd relocated to a small town not far from Coeur d'Alene in northern Idaho. Not long after Pete got out of prison, he was voted in as the Wolves' president. A few months later, Kull learned Vivian had died in some sort of auto accident. Kull's comment about her death played over and over in Del's mind.

"You ask me, it wasn't an accident."

Kull encouraged Del to dig up what he could, do his own investigation on Viv's death. After he met with Sheriff McNabb, he just might do that.

Amy sat cross-legged on the bed of her dingy motel room, studying the files for what felt like the millionth time. Page after page of notes, maps, newspaper clippings, and internet articles, everything she'd learned since her mother's death, lay before her.

She'd finished finals her junior year at Boise State and had begun packing for the drive home. Two calls to her mother had both gone to voicemail, which hadn't bothered Amy at the time. Her mother worked two jobs.

One clerking in a dry cleaning store, the other as night bartender at the Savage Wolves' clubhouse near a small town north of Coeur d'Alene. She made good money off the tips the Wolves gave her. Although she and Pete weren't living together, knowing she'd been his old lady provided her a certain amount of respect.

Amy had carried the last box outside, loading it into her car, when a Boise police cruiser pulled into the dormitory lot. She'd turned to go back inside when one of the officers called out to her, asking if she knew Amelia Peterson.

That was how she'd learned her mother's car had gone off the road, plunging down a ravine and flipping onto its side before coming to rest against the trunk of a large pine. Killed instantly was what Amy had been told, an instant before she'd fainted.

She'd never believed the theory her mother had been distracted and lost control. After all Amy had discovered over the years, she had no doubt her mother's death was no accident. If all went as planned, it wouldn't be long before she had enough evidence to prove it. All she had to do was stay alive.

The sound of her phone had Amy jumping off the bed, pulling it from her purse. Recognizing the name, she answered.

"How're you doing, baby girl?"

A smile curved her lips. "As good as you'd expect. I had a little scare this week."

"I heard. It's what I was afraid would happen if you started pushing hard on this. Any idea who set the fire?"

"Yeah, but I'm more concerned about how he found me. I've been so careful." Amy rubbed a couple fingers across her brow.

"Someone recognized you, maybe notified Pete. From what I heard, whoever started the fire used little accelerant. The arson investigator told Detective Zoeller she thought it was a prank, probably by teenagers."

Sitting down on the bed, she leaned back. "Is that what *you* believe?"

"Nope. I think it was set to scare you off. You know, baby girl, maybe it's time to give what you have to the police in Coeur d'Alene, let them finish it up."

They had this conversation before, and would probably have it again before her mother got the justice she deserved. The club had strong ties to the police in what they considered *their* town north of Coeur d'Alene. Rarely did they venture into the larger city, doing their best to stay below the radar.

"You know I can't do that. I doubt any police department would be inclined to take my information and go against another group of officers. They'd thank me, then file what I give them in a shredder." She blew out a frustrated breath. "I just don't know what to do."

"You have the answer to that right in front of you."

She shook her head. "I can't get him involved. What if whoever's trying to scare me off goes after him?"

"You're one woman against a group of people who know how to hide their tracks and bury the evidence. He has resources you can't begin to understand. Trust me, sweetheart. He'd do whatever he could to help you."

"Why? It's been years since we knew each other. Even then, we were just friends."

"You know why. That boy's been crazy about you since high school. And don't try to fool me, baby girl. I know you felt the same about him. If your mom hadn't warned you off, been afraid of what Pete would do if he knew you had a boyfriend, you would've been more than friends."

Amy agreed. "I'll think about it."

"Don't think too long. You've come this far. It'd be a shame if anything happened to you or your evidence before Vivian gets the justice she deserves."

"You're right."

A deep chuckle came over the phone. "Of course I am. Take care of yourself, baby girl."

A smile tugged at the corners of her mouth. "You, too, Uncle Kull."

"Have a seat, Del. Coffee?"

Sheriff Neville McNabb didn't wait for him to answer before signaling to his deputy. When the cups were set down, McNabb closed the door. Tall and lean, he'd been sheriff for twenty years, having no desire to take his pension any time soon.

Nev nodded toward a box next to his desk. "This is what I have on Peterson and the Savage Wolves. Even with all this documentation, the club is still somewhat of a mystery. You've got questions about Peterson. Well, so do most of the lawmen in this state. Anything specific you want to find out?"

Del thought of what he'd learned so far, knowing he had too many unanswered questions to narrow it down to a few. "How much time do you have?"

Nev chuckled, leaning back in his chair, cradling his coffee. "Why don't you start with something and we'll go from there?"

"Vivian Peterson."

The crinkles around Nev's eyes deepened as his gaze narrowed. "Peterson's old lady. Died a long time ago in some freak car accident up in Idaho. I heard she'd filed for divorce, but don't think it ever went through." Taking a sip from the cup, he focused on a spot behind Del, his attention drifting. "Viv and I went to high school together. Smart girl, real nice. I never knew what she saw in Pete, but once he went after her, no one else stood a chance."

"Did the two of you go out?"

His jaw tightened. "For a time our senior year. Then she met Pete. He was several years older, rode a motorcycle, and carried an attitude that turned everyone off...except the women." Nev shook his head. "The Savage

Wolves were in their infancy. I don't know if he just hung with them or was an actual prospect at the time. Later, I learned he'd become vice president, married Viv, and had a little girl."

"Amelia."

Nev's gaze shifted to Del. "That's right. As I recall, Vivian called her Amy." Setting down his cup, Nev rested his arms on the desk. "She moved the girl to Whiskey Bend for a while. Did you know her?"

Nodding, Del blew out a breath. "Same class in high school. We never dated, but were friends. She and her mother disappeared after our junior year. I never heard anything more about her and didn't realize, until recently, Peterson was her father."

One of Nev's brows lifted. "Why the curiosity now?"

"Last Monday, there was a fire at a small house a few blocks from my office. I drove over to see if I could help and spotted someone running away from the back of the place. Chased her for blocks, but she kept eluding me. When I finally caught her, turned out it was Amy Peterson." He shook his head, recalling his mistake in trusting she wouldn't run again. "I screwed up and she took off. Hurdled a fence like a damn gazelle and lost herself in a group of apartment buildings. Talked to the residents, searched the buildings. Nothing."

"And the fire?"

"Arson." Del scratched his forehead, leaning forward to rest his arms on his thighs. "The Amy I knew would never do something like that. It got me wondering. Did she set it? If so, why? Was someone after her? If that's the case, was the fire intended to scare or kill her? The police detective assigned to the case hasn't learned anything."

"So you thought you'd step in and lend a hand."

"Zoeller wouldn't be happy with me sticking my nose into it, but hell, I don't really care."

A bleak smile curved Nev's mouth. "I don't see a problem. You're an officer of the law who's trying to help an old friend. Nothing says you can't do a little investigating on your own."

"That's what I keep telling myself."

Standing, Nev opened a file drawer, digging around at the back until he pulled out a well-worn folder. Moving toward Del, he leaned a hip against his desk, handing it to him.

"I did the same when Vivian died. The accident happened on a pretty straight stretch of road. Clear day, no weather, middle of the afternoon, no traffic. When I heard about it, the car had already been recovered, towed away to a salvage yard. I got there the next morning. The lot owner had already run it through a car crusher. Local police figured it was an accident."

Del opened the folder, scanning through it. "You don't agree."

"Never did. I'd heard of problems within the Wolves. Dissension between Pete's club and the one in northern Idaho where Vivian worked as a bartender."

Del's brows rose. "No kidding?"

"Yeah. Of all the jobs she could've gotten, she chose to work for the Wolves." Straightening, Nev moved around his desk to sit down. "You want my guess?"

"I'll take whatever you can give me."

"Little Amelia Peterson is digging into something that should be left alone. Someone doesn't like it and is trying to scare her off."

A piece fell into place for Del. "She came by here asking questions, didn't she?"

"Three times over the last few years. I never showed her what I compiled." Nev nodded to the folder in Del's hand. "She's a smart girl with good instincts. My suggestion is for you to find Amy and convince her the past isn't worth risking her life."

The sun had begun to drop over the western mountains as Amy dumped out the last of the money she carried with her onto the bed. Counting her cash, she came up with a little over two hundred dollars. Enough to last three more nights in the low-rent motel with a little left over for food and gasoline. She needed to drive the short distance into Whiskey Bend and use her debit card to replenish her funds.

For the past year, she'd used an assumed name in an attempt to hide her actions from the person threatening her about investigating her mother's death. Almost eighteen months ago, he'd found her in southern Idaho, broke into her studio apartment, and left a detailed message of what would happen if she didn't stop digging into the crash. He'd scared Amy enough to halt her actions for a few months, giving her ample time to locate someone who provided fake identification, including a social security number, driver's license, and birth certificate. Thank goodness for Uncle Kull and his connections.

Falling back onto the bed, she laid an arm over her eyes. She wasn't even sure why she'd come back to Whiskey Bend, except the idea took root when she'd quietly returned for Mike Weiker's memorial service.

Growing up, it was the one place she'd felt safe, as if she had a future away from the strange world of her father. Uncle Kull still lived in town. He'd been a friend of her parents, keeping watch on Amy and her mother when they'd tried to leave the Savage Wolves behind.

Rolling to her side, she tucked her hands under her head and closed her eyes, letting an image of Del take shape. Honesty had always been important to Amy, as it had to her mother. The loss of trust had been why her mother snuck them out of White Basin during a club run to Bozeman. Perhaps that was why she couldn't pretend not to know the real reason she'd returned to Whiskey Bend.

Del Macklin had never left her thoughts. Not after her mother moved them to Idaho, or during her time in college, or during the years she'd been hunting her mother's killer. They'd never been on a date, never held hands, never kissed. In her fantasies, they'd done all of that and more. His friendship had meant a great deal to her during a lonely time in her life.

Amy had told herself repeatedly it had been a crush and nothing more. As a woman of thirty, she could no longer lie to herself. She'd come back to Whiskey Bend because of Del.

Unfortunately, the man tracking Amy had discovered her presence, probably been expecting her to return. If she did what Kull suggested and sought out Del's help, she might uncover enough evidence to arrest her mother's killer and obtain justice after all this time. It could also place him in danger.

Amy had wrestled with the pros and cons ever since Kull's call that morning, feeling no closer to a decision. Exhausted, she placed a hand on her stomach at the low growl. Getting out of her tiny motel room, finding a place to eat, and clearing her mind became a priority.

Picking up her purse, she stepped into the cool night air, already feeling some of her tension ease. She'd grab a burger, maybe even splurge for a chocolate shake, then return to her cramped room and start all over again.

Chapter Four

A multi-car accident stalled Del's return home by an extra hour. He'd planned to stop at Wicked Waters, talk to Kull, and see if his friend could shed more light on what Sheriff McNabb had given him. The delay had given him more time to think of Amy and all he'd learned about her since she left Whiskey Bend.

Del hadn't pushed Rick Zoeller for information on his investigation into the fire. He had been grateful for the little bit the detective volunteered. According to the landlord, he'd rented the house to a Susan Miller, a single woman, new to Whiskey Bend, who hadn't listed an employer. She'd volunteered to show him a modified statement of her savings account, showing more than enough funds to rent the house for quite a while.

As much as he hated to, Del advised Rick he'd identified Amelia Peterson as the person who ran from the fire. She matched the description of Susan Miller, leading them to conclude Amy was living under a fake identity. Del had no doubt Rick had already put steps in place to track her using any means necessary, including credit card charges and bank transactions.

Seeing the lights of a diner not far from Whiskey Bend, Del decided his empty stomach needed food before visiting Kull. Pulling to a stop in the parking lot, he reached for his hat, spotting a lone figure walking toward the building. Hesitating, he waited until the person got closer. When the wind picked up, catching the hoodie with enough force to whip it off their head, his breath hitched. Amy Peterson had just walked right back into his life.

Waiting until she'd stepped inside, he followed, watching her take a seat in a booth. When Amy held the menu up, he moved toward her, slipping into the bench seat across from her.

"Good evening, Amy."

The menu froze in place, then began to shake as she slowly lowered it, her eyes showing the same fear as when he'd stopped her during the fire.

Leaning forward, he rested his arms on the table. "You're supposed to say, *Good evening, Del. How are you doing?*"

Her lips twitched. Setting the menu down, she blew out a breath. "Good evening, Del. How are you doing?"

His eyes held the slightest bit of amusement. "A lot better since I saw you walk in here. I'm guessing you're as hungry as me, but before we order, there's something I need to get straight." He saw her gaze flicker to the door behind him. "Don't even think about it. You aren't lucky enough to get away from me twice."

Shoulders sagging, she nodded. "What do you need to get straight?" His answering grin tugged at her heart, reminding her of the boy she'd cared so much about, maybe even loved.

"Do I call you Susan Miller, or should I stick with Amelia Peterson?"

Shaking her head, Amy rubbed her right temple, pressing hard. "It isn't what you think, Del."

He opened his mouth to answer, then closed it when the waitress stepped up. "What can I get you, Sheriff?"

He glanced at Amy, who looked away. "Two cheeseburgers with fries. No onions. Everything else on the side. And two root beers."

"Coming right up."

As the waitress walked away, Amy's gaze shot to his. "Root beer?"

He tilted his head to the side, lifting a shoulder. "You used to drink them all the time in high school. Snuck them onto campus after they banned sodas."

Her eyes softened. "And the burger?"

"Did I get something wrong?"

Biting her lip, she shook her head. "No. You got it all perfect. I just can't believe you remembered after all this time."

It was his turn to look away, not wanting her to see more than she should. He had a job to do and a woman to take back to the office.

"Tell me about Susan." He could sense the tension rolling off her, wishing he could reach across the table to cover her hand with his. Instead, he leaned back, crossing his arms, surprised when she straightened her back, jutting out her chin.

"She's the only thing standing between me and the person who's after me."

Del didn't wait for more before signaling the waitress to wrap up their orders to go. Paying, he gripped Amy's arm, checking the lot before leading her outside and into the back of his car. Grabbing a pair of cuffs, he locked her hands in front of her, ignoring her hissed protest.

"Lay down on the seat. I don't want anyone recognizing you when we drive through town."

Climbing in, he glanced over his shoulder, relieved to see she'd done as he asked. As he started the engine, another thought took shape.

Instead of turning onto the highway toward Whiskey Bend, he went the opposite direction. After a while, he turned onto a well-packed dirt road several miles from town, following it until a rustic cabin came into view. Getting out, he opened her door, taking hold of her arm.

"Where are we?" She let him help her out, her eyes widening at the one story log structure with wrap-around porch and stone chimney.

He didn't answer as he led her onto the porch and unlocked the door. Stepping aside to usher her in, he turned to look at the surrounding area. Seeing nothing, he closed the door behind him, locked it, then flipped on a light. When he gripped her arm this time, she dug in her heels, refusing to budge.

Her eyes sparked as she looked up at him. "Where are we, Del?"

He studied her a minute, knowing he shouldn't trust her, realizing he would anyway. "It's my home away from home. No one knows about it except by brothers, Thorn and Boone, and Thorn's wife, Grace."

Her lips parted, a whoosh of air escaping. "He married Grace?"

Moving away, he took off his hat, setting it on the small dining table. "I forgot you knew about them in high school. You took off just before Thorn left."

"I didn't know he left."

"He enlisted in the army after Grace's father told him she'd left town. Seems to be a pattern with the women in the Macklin brothers' lives. Leaving, that is."

She felt a surge of heat rush through her at his comment, wondering if Del had considered her important to him in high school. Amy had never considered he'd miss her—not the way she'd missed him.

"Anyway, when he got out, Thorn returned home. They hooked-up not long after and now they're married." Walking into the kitchen, he flipped on another light. "Thirsty?"

Holding up her bound hands, she tilted her head.

"Not a chance those are coming off yet. You can hold your root beer with them like that." He pulled their drinks from the bag, along with their burgers and fries. "Have a seat." He nodded at the couch, waiting until she sat down before handing her the root beer.

Gripping it with both hands, she took a large swallow, then set it on the table. "What I really need is a bathroom."

"Down the hall."

Again, she held up her hands.

"Not a chance."

"You can't expect me to, well…do my business this way."

Del studied her. He'd already gone way outside protocol by bringing Amy to his cabin instead of depositing her with Detective Zoeller. The fact she'd run away from him once didn't help his trust factor.

"Sorry. You'll have to manage with the cuffs on."

The glare she sent him would've cowered him back in high school. Not anymore.

He watched as she walked down the hall, looking into a bedroom on the left, then into the bathroom on her right. Stepping inside, she turned on the light, slamming the door shut. Waiting a minute, he followed, leaning back against the wall, stifling a chuckle at the muffled curses he heard through the door. After a few minutes, the door flew open, a red-faced Amy scowling at him.

"I need your help."

His jaw dropped, mouth going dry when his gaze lowered to her jeans. She'd undone the button and slid down the zipper, a tiny piece of shiny, bright purple material peeking through the opening.

"My jeans are too tight to get over my hips with my hands like this. You have to either take these cuffs off or push down my pants."

The stupidity of the situation smacked him in the face. "I don't think—"

"I don't care what you think, Del Macklin. You got me into this mess, so the least you can do is help me. Please, I need to—"

He held up his hands, stopping her. "Fine. What do you want me to do?"

Turning around, Amy did her best to lift the bottom of her hoodie. "Pull my jeans down enough in the back so I can push them the rest of the way." She waited, expecting Del to get right to it. Glancing over her shoulder, she saw him still standing behind her, not moving. "Del...just do it."

He looked up, seeing the plea in her eyes, then back down at the bare spot at the small of her back. He'd undressed plenty of women before taking them to bed and never blinked an eye. Those women never had his heart pounding in a ferocious rhythm or caused his forehead and the palms of his hands to dampen.

Wiping them down his pants, he stepped forward, gripping her jeans with his fingers before slowly pulling them down, mumbling a low curse when he saw evidence of a thong.

Again, Amy looked over her shoulder. "What did you say?"

Del shook his head. "Nothing."

He did his best not to look, then his fingers brushed Amy's skin. Letting go, he stepped away, as if he'd been singed.

Frustrated, Amy let out a deep breath. "Now what?"

Hardening his jaw, forcing his mind to clear, he gripped her pants once more and gave a hard tug. His gaze zeroed in on the two rounds of creamy skin for an instant before she moved into the bathroom, slamming the door behind her. Falling back against the wall, he forced his body to relax.

He let his breathing calm before pushing away and starting toward the living room.

"Del?"

Turning, pulling his gaze away from the bathroom door where a thin ray of light streamed out, he lifted his head. "What?"

"Am I going to be sleeping here tonight?"

He shoved away images of her in his bed before answering. "Yes."

"Can I borrow a shirt? One that buttons up the front."

That he could do. "Hold on."

The bathroom door remained closed as he walked past it and into his bedroom. Yanking an older chambray shirt from a hanger, he took the few steps back to the bathroom door.

"Here it is."

When the door opened, Amy stood in front of him, her jeans in a heap in the corner, her slender legs more enticing than he could have ever imagined.

Smirking, she watched the path of his gaze. "It will be easier this way."

Nodding, he held out the shirt.

"You need to take off the cuffs so I can slip it on."

This time, he saw no way around it, wishing he'd simply taken them off when they first arrived at the cabin. Reaching into his pocket, he pulled out the key.

"Hold out your hands."

An instant later, he felt a wave of guilt as she rubbed her wrists. Even though the department used the latest design, if someone tugged at them, trying to get free, the cuffs could still cause redness and, at times, swelling.

"Thank you." She shut the door again. No more than a minute passed before she stepped into the hall.

Even under the circumstances, Amy had never looked more beautiful, or more tempting. It would take every bit of his willpower to control the situation, not giving in to what he wanted. Clearing his throat, he pointed toward the sofa.

"If you're cold, you can use the blanket folded on the back." He moved to the fireplace, started a fire, then stood. Turning, he saw she'd wrapped the blanket around her legs, curling up at one end of the sofa, her eyes drifting shut. Walking to her, he drew a finger down her cheek.

"Are you hungry?"

Shaking her head, she closed her eyes again.

"Sorry, but you can't go to sleep until you've told me what's going on."

Nodding, she sat up. Looking at the burger on the table, she unwrapped it and took a bite, chasing it with her root beer.

Del followed her lead, devouring his meal in seconds. Picking up his drink, he sat back in the chair across from her, waiting.

Taking her time, Amy finished the burger and fries, crushing the paper. Clearing her throat, she began her story.

Del didn't take notes and rarely interrupted as Amy's voice altered between anger, fear, frustration, and pain. More than anything, he wanted to wrap his arms around her, tell her everything would work out. He didn't. Doing so could give her false hope, and right now, he didn't know how much of her story was true and how much was what she chose to believe.

What struck him was the consistency of her story when compared to what he'd learned from Nev McNabb, Kull, Joe Nolen, and his own research. Neither McNabb nor Kull believed Vivian's death was accidental, yet no one could come up with a motive.

By all accounts, she'd grown up in a tight-knit family, had been a good student and a cheerleader with lots of friends. Her life changed when she met Pete. Although she still visited her parents, she lost track of all her friends from high school, or more accurately, they chose to have nothing to do with her after she'd chosen a life inside a biker gang.

"Mom and Dad seemed happy, always holding hands, laughing." Amy paused, clasping her hands together to stop them from shaking. "Then this new chick showed up at the club. The other old ladies warned Mom about her, said she was trouble, but Mom didn't listen."

Amy glanced up at Del. "She trusted him, you know? After all those years, he'd never pulled some of the stuff the other members did with their old ladies. One day, she showed up at the club to pick up some stuff and found them. Dad kept a private room at the clubhouse, as did a few other members. He was in bed with the skank Mom had been warned about. According to her, Mom didn't say a word when he yelled for her to stop. She drove home, packed, picked me up from school, swung by the bank, and never looked back. Wouldn't take his calls, refused to see him when he showed up at the house in Whiskey Bend." She swiped at a tear. "Mom never got over it. And it was my fault."

Del grabbed a tissue from a nearby box, handing it to her before tilting his head. "How could that have been your fault?"

Using the tissue, she wiped her eyes, then crumbled it in her fist. "I met the woman when some friends and I stopped for sodas after school. She didn't have a place to go, had hung around a club in Idaho, and was looking for a place to stay. I told her my dad was with a club and she should check them out. If I'd only known…"

Leaving his chair, Del took a seat on the sofa, putting an arm around her to draw her close. "It was your father's choice, Amy, not yours. He could've refused what she offered, but he didn't. Vivian left Pete because he betrayed her, not because of anything you did."

Settling her head under his chin, she nodded. "Mom said the same thing."

Del drew back, looking down at her, arching a brow.

"About a year after moving to Whiskey Bend, she got drunk and finally told me what happened with Dad. The thing is, Mom never drank. Not at club parties, at home, or when she and Dad went out. She always said he drank enough for both of them. Anyway, she filed for divorce. Dad was served, but didn't sign. Instead, he put the papers in an envelope and mailed them to Mom, the word *NEVER* scrawled across the top page. He included nothing else. No apology, no note saying he still loved her and wanted to work it out. Nothing."

Del kissed her forehead. "Then he was arrested and went to prison."

Amy nodded. "That was the only other time I saw her drink. This time, though, she sat in the living room sipping wine. It was the end of our junior year."

"Yeah, I remember you not answering my calls or showing up at any of the parties over the summer."

Looking up, she kissed his jaw, then rested her head on his shoulder. "I'm so sorry about that. She'd already made the decision to move us to Coeur d'Alene. I refused, telling her I had one year left and intended to graduate in Whiskey Bend. That's when she showed me the note."

Del stilled, trying to remember anyone mentioning a note before now. "What note?"

"Someone in the club blamed her for Dad and another member going to prison. It said they knew she had talked to the Feds, given them false information to get back at him for what he did."

"Did she?"

Amy pushed away, her eyes haunted as they focused on his. "Never. She hated what he did, but never stopped loving him. Besides, everyone in the club knew not to discuss business with anyone outside of patched members, including old ladies. Even if she had wanted to get back at him, she had no story to tell."

He tightened his hold, drawing Amy back down to his chest. "Who signed the note?"

"No signature. Mom thought she recognized the writing, but never told me a name. Anyway, it ended with a threat. Mom believed she had no choice but to leave."

"She did the right thing, Amy. Keeping you safe became her priority."

"You know, she did go see him in prison one time. I'd graduated from high school and was headed to Boise for college. Even though Mom never said as much, I knew my father provided the money for tuition and for me to stay in a dorm."

"Is that why she went to see him? To thank him for being a dad?" Del couldn't help the tinge of sarcasm.

"Maybe. I don't really know. She took him an envelope filled with pictures of me. Mom said it was the first time she'd ever seen his eyes cloud with tears. It had been about four years since she'd walked out, since I'd seen him. Maybe he did miss me a little."

Del stroked her head, letting his fingers thread through her hair, not responding. After a few minutes, she continued.

"He told her never to visit him again. They were done and he wanted nothing more do with her…or me." She took a shuddering breath, brushing away more tears. "I don't think Mom expected much from him, but what he said destroyed whatever feelings she still had. She didn't tell me any of this until the following summer when I came home before my sophomore year. It's funny. Even when you know your dad has done terrible things, it's still hard to hate him. He was my father and I wanted to love him. Hearing the devastation in Mom's voice when she told me what he'd said, I couldn't help but hate him."

Del thought of the threatening note Vivian received in Whiskey Bend. "Did she ever receive another note or more threats against the two of you?"

"Yes, but I didn't find them until after she died." Amy jerked up, standing, letting the blanket fall to the floor. "What have I been thinking? All my notes, everything I've accumulated about her death is back at the motel. I have to go get them." She ran to the bathroom, coming out with her jeans and slipping them on. "Del, we have to go. Now."

Chapter Five

Del didn't bother with the cuffs as he settled Amy in the back seat of the car. Again, he told her to lay down. When he made it to the motel, he circled the building twice, looking for anyone who might be watching her room, then parked in back. He didn't like the place, knew it rented by the hour, as well as the night. It was the type of place people stayed when they wanted to remain anonymous.

Keeping her close to his side, he didn't rush as they walked around front, disappearing inside her room. Flipping on the light, he heard her let out a relieved sigh.

"Does everything look the same as when you left?"

Nodding, she dashed to the dresser, opening a drawer to pull a binder from under her clothes. Rifling through it, she sat down on the bed.

"It's all here." Reaching out, she searched the back of another drawer, grabbing the pouch with the rest of her money, then stood. "It won't take me long to pack."

Del walked around, trying to fathom the Amy he knew years ago being the woman who lived in this room. Although the rug was threadbare, the walls in need of fresh paint, and the bedspread so old, the printed pattern had disappeared, the place was clean. Out of curiosity, he lifted the bedspread, spotting the edge of a computer poking out between the mattress and box spring.

"I assume you want to take this with you." He grabbed the laptop, setting it on the bed.

"Yes. And everything else, which isn't much." Amy stopped, turning toward him. "I don't want to impose on you, Del. I should find another place to stay."

Snorting, he sat down on the edge of the bed. "Amy, you're a person of interest in an arson fire. I *should* deliver you to the police station and let them sort out what to do next."

Shoving aside her fear, she took a couple steps toward him. "Are you going to? Take me to the police, I mean."

Scrubbing a hand down his face, Del shook his head. "Not tonight. You'll stay with me at the cabin. Tomorrow, I want to go over your entire story again."

Crossing her arms, she moved away to lean against the dresser. "Suppose I don't want to stay with you?"

Standing, he stepped to within a few inches of her, leaning down. "Then you'd leave me no choice but to introduce you to Rick Zoeller, the detective in charge of investigating the fire. Your accommodations wouldn't be as nice as my guest room, but if that's what you want..." He let the implication hang, waiting for her to make a decision.

Shifting her gaze away, she shook her head. "I didn't start the fire, Del. Whoever is threatening me is the one who set it."

"Then give me the information I need to talk with Zoeller. I don't have a choice about bringing him into this, Amy. I just want you to be prepared when we meet with him."

Swallowing the fear his words created, she stepped around him to grab a bag from the tiny closet. Stuffing her clothes inside, she moved to the bathroom, jamming the rest of her belongings into the remaining space. Last, she slid the laptop into its case.

"I'm ready."

Grabbing her bag, he stepped outside, holding up his hand. "Let me look around." After walking around the entire building, he got into his car, pulling to a stop in front of the room.

Amy climbed inside, closing the back door as he pulled from the lot. Once they were a couple miles away, she leaned forward, resting a hand on his shoulder.

"Thanks for at least listening to my side of things. Uncle Kull said I could trust you."

Del hit the brakes, feeling Amy's fingers dig into his shoulder, then heard her gasp as she fell back against the seat. Maneuvering the car off the road and to a stop, he shifted in his seat, looking behind him. "*Uncle* Kull?"

"Geez. You could give a girl some warning."

"How do you know Kull?"

She looked at him as if he'd grown horns. "He and Pete have been friends forever. When we moved to Whiskey Bend, he'd come over sometimes, bring extra food, keep Mom company. He's the one who introduced me to the owner of the house I was staying at before the fire. Why?"

Del pinched the bridge of his nose. "I'm going to throttle him," he mumbled before turning away, thinking he should turn the car around and head straight to Wicked Waters.

"What is it, Del?"

He let out a breath, pulling back onto the highway, wondering what else he didn't know. "My brothers and I met Kull before high school. I still stop by Wicked Waters at least twice a week to have dinner and talk with him. I even asked him about you." Gripping the steering wheel tighter, he stared straight ahead. "He never *once* mentioned he was a friend of the family." Turning off the highway onto the dirt road leading to the cabin, he glanced in the rearview mirror, lifting a brow. "Kull and your mother. They never..."

"Of course not. He was a friend, supported Mom when everyone in the club turned away because of their loyalty to my father. Uncle Kull is the only person who believes in me."

Parking, he leaned his head back against the seat. "I always believed in you, Amy. Even when you left without letting me know, I still thought you'd be back one day." He didn't wait for her response before climbing out and opening the back door. Picking up her bag with one hand, he extended the other toward her.

Taking it, Amy held her laptop close to her side as they walked to the front door. When they stepped inside, she set down the computer, not letting go of his hand, gripping it so he turned to face her.

"I'm sorry I didn't reach out to you, Del. I wish it hadn't happened as it did, but Mom was scared. I'd never seen her so frightened, even when Pete went on rides she knew were dangerous. She made me promise not to contact anyone." She placed her other hand on his arm. "If it's any consolation, I missed you more than anyone, even my father."

Bringing his hand up to her face, he stroked his fingers down her cheek, brushing her bottom lip with his thumb. Moving his hand to the back of her neck, he drew her close, leaning down.

"I missed you, too," he whispered before lowering his mouth to hers.

The simple touch of her lips to his set off an internal reaction he'd never felt with another woman. Heat rushed through him, as if he'd been thrust into a burning building. Only this burn didn't hurt.

As he deepened the kiss, tasting her in a way he'd done only in his dreams, she wrapped her arms around his neck, not allowing him to pull away. His hands moved across her back, settling on her hips, drawing her close so her body aligned with his. Her small whimpers did nothing to cool the flame spreading through him.

The building sensations felt too good to be wrong, even if the timing couldn't be worse. Drawing back, he rested his forehead against hers, sucking in a ragged breath. Touching her face, he lifted a strand of hair, tucking it behind her ear before kissing her once more, then stepping away.

"It's been a long day for both of us. We should get some sleep."

Her face flushed, lips damp, she picked up her computer in one hand, bag in the other, and walked down the hall. She didn't reach the guest bedroom before Del's hand settled on her shoulder, turning her to face him.

"We'll get through this, Amy. Find whoever is threatening you and put them away. Once that's done, you and I are going to have a long talk that has nothing to do with the past. We'll focus on the future. You with me on this?"

For the first time since he'd seen her after the fire, she smiled. Not the full-on type that brightened her entire face and twisted his heart in high school, but still a smile. Nodding, she leaned up, kissing his cheek.

"I'm with you."

Amy pulled the covers under her chin, wishing sleep would claim her. After two hours, she had a hard time calming the sensations pulsing through her. She could still feel Del's kiss, the way the hard muscles of his chest felt against her as he pulled her close.

She had other lovers. One before her mother died, during her junior year in college. That ended when she left college to return to Coeur d'Alene. Another one a couple years later while working as an office manager during the day, spending her nights searching for her mother's killer. It lasted a few months, until he figured out her priorities weren't focused on him.

The last one happened out of sheer loneliness. Amy had moved again, taking a job in a family-owned restaurant near Billings, hoping to connect with members of the local Savage Wolves club.

One of the restaurant suppliers had asked her to join him for drinks. Afterward, they'd gone to his place. It had been quick and unfulfilling. Every time she thought of it, she felt a little emptier, wishing she'd never gone with him in the first place. She'd stayed at the job another week before realizing she didn't have the contacts to learn more.

There'd been no one else, and none had made her feel like Del did with tonight's kiss. She'd meant what she said. Once they got through this, cleared her name and found her mother's killer, Amy would do whatever it took to make things work with Del.

"Hey, sleepyhead. Are you going to stay in bed all day?"

Amy's eyes opened to slits, a stream of bright light hitting her face as Del pulled back the curtains. Grabbing the covers, she pulled them over her head, hearing him chuckle.

"It's a little after eight. Time to get up and dressed." He pulled the covers back. "We have a lot to do today."

He held out a cup of steaming coffee. "Sorry, but I don't know what you take in it." He nodded toward the table by the bed where he'd placed sugar and a small pitcher of milk.

Sitting up, she took the cup, adding both sugar and milk. "How long have you been up?"

"Since five. I don't need much sleep. You, on the other hand..."

"It's true. I'm a lightweight when it comes to sleep. I need seven or eight hours, more if I can make it happen."

Del smiled. "Get dressed and meet me in the kitchen. I'll get breakfast ready."

Leaving her alone, he walked to the table where both their laptops sat. Picking up her binder, he flipped through it once more. He'd read each page, studied every photograph, his gut clenching at much of what she'd written. Del wondered if she knew how close she was to identifying the killer.

"What's for breakfast?"

He looked up when she slipped her arms around his waist, pressing her chest to his back. Setting the binder aside, he turned toward her, dropping a quick kiss onto her lips. Doing more would only delay what they needed to discuss.

"Eggs, bacon, toast…fruit if you want it."

Her stomach growled. "Guess I'd better take it all."

She leaned against the counter, enjoying the sight of him cooking. Within fifteen minutes, their plates were full, Amy not waiting to sit down before grabbing a piece of bacon.

With the table loaded with their laptops and her binder, they sat on the sofa, setting their plates on the coffee table. He watched her take several bites before turning toward her, resting an arm across the back of the sofa.

"I read your notes."

"Yeah, I figured you would." She took another slice of bacon, chewing it slowly.

"Seems to me you're close to identifying who killed your mother."

"The best I've been able to do is narrow it down to four people." She dropped the strip of bacon back onto her plate. "Four people, Del. I can't get any closer than that."

"Have you thought about the motive for each one?"

She cocked her head to the side. "Such as?"

"Such as what did each of them have to gain by killing your mother? And how would threatening you help them now?"

Leaning her head against the back of the sofa, she closed her eyes. A few minutes later, she shook her head.

"I don't know for sure, but I'm certain my father played a role in it. Either he ordered it done or he did it himself."

Crossing his arms, Del leaned back next to her. "What did Pete have to gain by killing Vivian? I'm sorry, sweetheart, but I can't think of anything. Even though he refused to sign the divorce documents, Pete told her he never wanted to see either of you again. From what you know, she respected his wishes and stayed away. Did Pete continue to pay for your college after her death?"

"I never went back. He continues to deposit money into my checking account each month, but I don't touch it. The first year, I moved it into a savings account, using what I earned to pay my bills. After I got the first threatening letter, I pulled most of it out to use as Susan Miller."

"Is he still sending you money?"

"Into the same account every month. I just don't touch it."

Drawing in a slow breath, Del let it out, shaking his head. "I know you hate him, Amy, but it doesn't make sense to me. Have you talked to him since your mother died?"

"No."

Del heard the slight tremor in her voice. "Did he ever try to reach out, want to meet?" He felt her stiffen next to him. "Amy?"

"A few times. He left messages on my phone. When I changed numbers, he sent letters. I ignored all of them." Her eyes were moist when she looked over at him. "He didn't even come to the funeral. I guess he couldn't be bothered."

"Maybe." Del still couldn't shake the sense someone else killed her mother. Getting up, he grabbed the binder, looking back through it until he found what he wanted. Sitting back down, he placed it in front of her. "Look here. You have an article about the killing of two Savage Wolves outside a bar in White Basin. That's where your father's club is located, right?"

"His chapter is."

"No witnesses, no other bikers around. The bartender said the men were drinking, went out back, and he found the bodies at closing. Did you ever follow-up to see if they found out who killed them?"

She scrunched her eyes, shaking her head. "No. Do you think it's important?"

"I don't know. What I'm saying is you have a ton of good information. You need to have someone who knows what they're doing go through it, sort the good from the bad. I can't help but think that if your mother really was murdered, you've got the killer in this binder." He flipped to some other pages, pointing to notes she had written. "How did you learn about this?"

She read a few lines, knowing what it said. "I don't know…"

"We've got to start somewhere, and this seems to be where you started getting to the heart of what happened."

Sitting up, she settled the notebook in her lap, recalling the time less than two years ago.

"I'd moved east of Missoula, taking a chance Pete or one of the Savage Wolves wouldn't spot me. I needed to be close to the club, talk to people who might have information about what happened to Mom. It wasn't hard to get a job in a bar frequented by bikers. My hair was a little longer then. I dyed it black, kept it in a loose ponytail, letting the front strands frame my face. Colored contacts turned my eyes from green to brown. Even I didn't recognize myself when I looked in the mirror."

Amy leaned forward, grabbing one more piece of bacon, quietly chewing it while she thought about how to tell Del the rest. Picking up her cold coffee, she took a sip, wincing at the taste.

"What happened at the bar?"

Del's question forced her to continue.

"After less than a month, I finally got a break. A member from the White Basin chapter came into the bar with a few others. I didn't recognize them and knew they'd have no idea I was the daughter of their club president. I switched tables with another waitress, bringing them drinks, letting them get a little touchy before moving out of reach. Close to two in the morning, the one who'd flirted with me the most grabbed my hand, pulling me through the back door and to the parking lot. He was pretty drunk, but something told me to go with him, maybe get him to talk." She paused a moment, choosing her next words, doing her best not to look at Del. "I knew what he wanted from me, but hoped I could get something from him first. He shoved me against the outside wall, groping, kissing. I was able to get my hands between us and push him back. For whatever reason, he laughed, taking it as a challenge. When he came toward me again, he stumbled, landing on his hands and knees. I wanted to run. Instead, I reached down to help him up."

Glancing at Del, she could see the stone-cold look on his face, his jaw hard, a muscle twitching. "It was the best thing I could've done. He sat down on an old bench and started talking. Said I looked just like a picture in the clubhouse of the president's old lady. Then he went on to tell me she'd died in some freak auto accident. He laughed, making me want to slap him. Somehow, I stayed silent. He said some of the older brothers never believed it was an accident. He mumbled something about them knowing what happened and why, then he laid his head down and passed out."

Amy closed the binder. She couldn't meet Del's gaze, didn't want to see the censure in his face at her method of getting information. A few seconds passed before she felt his hand under her chin, turning it so she had to look at him.

"That was incredibly stupid...and incredibly brave." Wrapping his arms around her, he kissed her, stroking her hair. Drawing back, he locked his gaze on hers. "And I never want to hear of you ever doing it again."

A nervous laugh escaped as she nodded. "Never again. Got it."

"We need to head into Whiskey Bend, Amy."

Her gaze shifted away, but not soon enough for her to hide the fear in her eyes.

"It'll be all right. Detective Zoeller is a good cop. If anyone can sort through this, find out what really happened, it's Rick."

Chapter Six

Del pulled to a stop in the police station parking lot, glancing at Amy, who hadn't said a word since leaving the cabin. Instead of hiding in the back, she sat in front with him. When she'd asked about bringing her bag and computer, he'd told her to leave them. Even if Rick decided to arrest her, Del would post bail and get her out before nightfall.

Walking around the car, he opened her door, holding out his hand, relieved when she grasped it. She didn't let go as they entered the station, her grip tightening a little when the officer on duty greeted Del.

"Hey, Del." The woman's gaze shifted to Amy, her eyes widening at their joined hands before she looked back at Del.

"Good morning, Lucy. Is Detective Zoeller available?"

"Let me check." She didn't pick up the phone, choosing to walk the short distance to his office. "Rick, Sheriff Macklin is here to see you. He, um…has a woman with him."

He shuffled a stack of folders to one side of his desk, not missing the odd inflection in Lucy's voice. Rick had heard rumors of the brief affair she had with Del, figuring it was long over. The look on her face told him he might be wrong.

"Do you want me to bring them back?"

"No thanks, Lucy. I'll get them." Standing, he followed her to the front, extending his hand to Del. "I've been meaning to call you about the latest on the fire."

Taking Rick's hand, he turned toward Amy. "That's why we're here. Rick, this is Amelia Peterson. Amy, this Detective Zoeller."

Amy lifted her chin, determined not to come off as weak or nervous. "Detective Zoeller, it's a pleasure." She held out her hand, glad when he took it without hesitating. "I've some things to tell you, including what I know of the fire on Monday. Do you have time to speak with me?"

"I've been waiting for the chance, Miss Peterson. Come back to my office. You, too, Del."

"As if I'd stay behind." Del chuckled, glancing at Lucy, seeing the question in her eyes. "We'll talk later." He headed into Rick's office.

"Coffee, water?" He gestured to the two empty chairs across from his desk.

Amy shook her head. "Nothing for me."

Del did the same, reluctantly letting go of her hand.

"All right then, Miss Peterson. I'm sure the sheriff has told you that you're a person of interest in the arson fire at your residence."

"Yes."

"Well, I appreciate you coming in on your own. This is a voluntary visit, correct?"

She tugged on the hem of her top, nodding. "Yes. Del didn't force me to come."

"Good. If you don't mind, I'm going to take notes. Why don't you start at the beginning? Take as long as you need and don't leave anything out. I want a complete picture of what led up to the fire."

Amy clasped her hands in her lap, took a quick glance at Del, then began.

Two hours later, Rick dropped his pen, rubbing the back of his neck. "It's quite a story. Do you have anything to substantiate what you've told me?"

"All her notes are in the back seat of my car. I'll go get them." Del stood, giving her a reassuring grin before he left to retrieve her binder.

"I'm guessing you've known the sheriff a long time."

Tearing her gaze away from Del's retreating back, she looked at Rick. "Yes. We were in the same class in high school. We were pretty good friends until my mother decided we had to move at the end of my junior year."

"Because of the threat?"

She bit her lip, nodding. "It wasn't easy to leave Whiskey Bend or Del."

"Here you go." Del set the binder on Rick's desk. "That's the one and only copy of the information she's collected since her mother died. The original threatening letter Vivian received is near the front."

Rick's brows lifted, his gaze moving to Amy. "The one that triggered your move from Whiskey Bend?"

"Mom kept everything hidden in a box under her bed. It's the first thing I retrieved when they told me she'd died."

"Here you are, Rick." Lucy walked into the office, depositing a bag from Evie's on his desk. She looked at Del. "You know where the drinks are. I've got to leave for a presentation at the school." Her gaze lingered on Del a few moments before she walked out. It was long enough for Amy to notice.

Rick focused on the information in the binder, not looking up. "Go ahead and get what you want to drink. Grab me a water, would you, Del?"

"Sure. Come on, Amy. You probably need to stretch, get the kinks out of your neck."

Following him to the employee lounge, she glanced over her shoulder, seeing Lucy walk outside. "Did she go to school with us?"

"Who?"

"The officer who just left."

"Lucy Ortiz? No. She moved here with her husband while I was away at college. What do you want to drink?" Reaching into the refrigerator, he pulled out a water for Rick, a soda for himself, then hesitated when Amy didn't answer. "Amy?"

"Sorry. Soda is fine." Taking it, she popped the tab, taking a long swallow.

He tapped a finger to her temple. "What's going on in that head of yours?"

"What? Oh, nothing."

"You never could lie. What's up?"

She felt heat creep up her neck and onto her cheeks. "Do you know her well?"

The can stilled at his lips. Lowering it, he debated a split second before telling her the truth. "Yes, I do. I helped her out when her abusive husband wouldn't accept their divorce. We started seeing each other. It didn't last long and has been over for a couple years." His gaze narrowed on hers. "Is that what you wanted to know?"

Amy felt embarrassed, digging into his private life when she had no right. "Yeah, I guess it is." She walked back to Rick's office, noticing Del didn't follow right away. Turning, she saw him on his phone, his back to her.

"Pick whatever sandwich you want, Miss Peterson."

Amy looked at Rick, glad for the opportunity to get her mind off Del. "I'd really like you to call me Amy or Amelia."

A warm smile spread across his face. "I'm kind of partial to Amelia." He pulled out a card, jotting something on the back. "Keep this with you. Call me anytime, day or night. My personal number is on the back."

Del stopped outside the office, hearing the brief exchange. If he hadn't gotten to know Rick, he would've thought the man was hitting on his girl. *His girl.* The words caused a jolt of longing to pass through him. He knew, without a doubt, Amy was who he wanted. No other woman had come close, and this time around, he meant to let her know. He'd been too timid in high school to take a chance, tell her how he felt. Those insecurities couldn't play a part in whatever happened between them now. Del figured he'd get one more chance with her, and he planned to make the most of it.

Sitting down, he set Rick's water in front of him, then took the last sandwich in the bag. Ham and cheese on sourdough, as if he'd ordered it himself. He took a large bite.

"Have you read through this binder, Del?" Rick picked up his water, twisting off the cap.

Swallowing, he nodded. "Twice this morning. My opinion is Amy has gone as far as she can. Pushing any more could endanger her even more. The fire was a warning. Who knows what will happen next time."

Rick reread her notes about the night she'd spoken with the drunk biker and his remark about it not being an accident. "From all you've said this morning, I gather you believe your father was involved in your mother's death."

Amy took a sidelong glance at Del, nodding. "I can't come up with anyone else, but Del's right. There was no real motive for Pete to kill Mom." Setting her sandwich down, she rubbed her eyes with the palms of her hands, pressing to relieve the tension. "Have you ever known something in your heart, but couldn't prove it?"

Rick snickered. "All the time."

"Well, that's where I'm at. I know my mother was killed. She'd driven that road a hundred times in all conditions—snow, wind, torrential rain—and never had an accident. How could this happen on a clear day with little traffic? And why did the police rush to destroy her car before a real investigation could take place? Then there are all the hostile notes. Why would someone threaten me, tell me to back off, unless they knew she'd been murdered? You've seen what I have. What do you think?"

Leaning back in his chair, Rick looked between her and Del, letting out a weary breath. "I think you've got the foundation for further investigation into your mother's death. I'm going to make some calls, see what else I can learn. It will take some time. Is there a place you can stay where you'll be safe?"

"I—"

"Amy's staying with me."

Rick's eyes flickered in amusement. "I thought as much."

"And the arson fire?" Del asked.

"An open investigation, for now. Amy, I don't want you to leave the area without letting me know. And definitely do not do any more digging on your own. If someone contacts you, threatens you, let Del know, then come straight here. Understand?"

Amy nodded.

Rick's face softened. "You've had a rough few years. Take some time off, try to relax and have some fun. I'll put whatever time I can into this, but you must let me do my job."

Again, Amy nodded, fighting the tears of relief.

Standing, Del reached for her hand. "No problem, Rick. Call me if something turns up or if you need my help. You've got my cell."

Rick stood, holding out his hand to Del. "Trust me. I won't hesitate to use it."

Amy didn't know how she felt about being cut out of the search for her mother's killer. The hunt had consumed her for so long, she felt adrift without it. She didn't have a job or a place to live, and couldn't allow herself to hope something with Del might be permanent. At least Rick had decided to do what he could, which was more than she had going for her the last few years.

Facing straight ahead as Del drove toward the cabin, she licked her dry lips. "I guess it's time to look for a job and a new place to live." Amy hesitated before continuing. "The rented house was temporary until the landlord's aunt moved to town. I was thinking about one of the apartments around the corner from Gray Wolf Outfitters."

A muscle in Del's jaw ticked as his chest tightened. "The apartments where you lost me after the fire."

"Yeah. It's a big place. I'm guessing they have vacancies all the time." She continued to stare straight ahead, her mind moving in too many directions at once.

He slowed the car, making the turn onto the dirt road leading to his cabin. "There's no need to rush into anything. You're welcome to stay at my place as long as you want." Stopping in front, he shut off the engine, turning to face her. "If you want space, I can stay in town."

She cocked her head, her forehead creasing. "Who would you stay with?"

The corners of his mouth tilted into a grim smile. "No one, Amy. I own a house in town, which is where I stay most of the time. The cabin is where I come on weekends to get away."

"I just thought—"

"Yeah, I know what you thought. Let's get you settled before I go to the office for a few hours. While I'm gone, take a bath, read a book, relax. You could make a list of things you need. When I get back, we'll run errands and grab dinner. Sound okay to you?"

She nodded, exhaling a relieved breath. "Sounds great." Getting out of the car, she followed him to the door, entering when he stepped aside.

"Cell service can be real iffy out here. I know it's old school, but if you can't get reception, there's a landline in the kitchen and one in my bedroom. If you need anything, call." He pulled a card from his pocket, jotting his cell number on the back. "Here. I know you already have Rick's information. Call and let him know he can reach you here. I'm planning to see Kull while in town. I'll let him know where you are."

Stepping next to him, she placed a hand on his arm. "Don't be angry with him, Del. He's been good to me, and I know how much he cares about you. If he didn't, he never would've told me to trust you."

Lifting her hand, he placed a kiss on her wrist, then another on her lips. "I'd better go. Try to relax and don't worry." She gave a slight nod, not meeting his gaze. "I'll be back in a few hours."

Looking out the front window, Amy watched him leave, a sense of loneliness enveloping her. Since her mother died, she'd seldom had time to feel alone. It was a new and unwelcome sensation.

Slipping her phone from her purse, she called Rick. He wasn't in the office, so she left her number and the phone number of the cabin with Del's friend, Lucy. The officer sounded a little surprised when Amy told her she'd be staying there, but didn't comment further, assuring her Rick would get the information.

Opening her laptop, she checked email, then stared at the screen, reminding herself Rick would take over where she left off. No longer was there a need for her to spend hours trying to figure out the puzzle that had consumed her life since she left college.

Finding a job became her new priority. Pulling up a local job board, she began to look, surprised at the number of openings listed in such a small town. The one with the most, Gray Wolf Outfitters, had ten openings in various departments. Surely, she had to be qualified for one of them.

An hour later, Amy had her résumé updated. Clicking their website, she found the employment section and uploaded her information, attaching her résumé. Feeling a small sense of accomplishment, she closed the laptop. Del's suggestion of a bath sounded real good right now. Only a glass of wine would make it seem perfect.

Searching the refrigerator, she found a half-full bottle of merlot. Fifteen minutes later, she reclined in a tub of hot water, a glass in one hand, her other arm behind her head. Taking a sip, she set the glass down, closing her eyes. Amy couldn't recall the last time she shouldered such a light burden. Her only regret was wishing she'd come back to Whiskey Bend, and Del, much sooner.

Chapter Seven

Del stepped into Wicked Waters, scanning the large Friday evening crowd, not seeing Kull anywhere. Walking to the end of the bar, he leaned against it, ordering a beer.

"If you're looking for Kull, he's finishing up an order in the back." The bartender nodded toward the hall, then pointed across the room. "The table in the corner is full of guys he was in the service with. They're on some kind of motorcycle trip to Idaho."

Del took the bait. "Which means?"

"They've been waiting almost an hour to talk to Kull about him joining them on the trip. On top of it being Friday, he may not have much time to talk to you. My suggestion is you head to his office, speak to him while he's working on the order. Once he gets back out here, well...good luck."

On a normal day, Del would've left, returning when his friend wasn't so busy. There wasn't anything normal about today.

Straightening, Del gripped his beer, tilting it toward the bartender. "Thanks."

"Hey. Just remember it the next time I get pulled over, Sheriff."

Shaking his head, Del chuckled as he walked down the hall, pushing through the door to Kull's office.

Looking up from a stack of papers, he motioned to a chair filled with empty boxes. "Set those on the floor and have a seat. I'll just be another couple minutes."

He did as Kull asked, settling into an old wooden office chair on the other side of the desk. Leaning back, Del tipped the bottle, taking a slow swallow, his gaze taking in the crowded shelves and walls overloaded with framed photos, most hanging at irregular angles. By the time his gaze returned to Kull, he'd set his paperwork aside, his arms resting on the desk.

"I wondered how long it would take you to get here."

Del's eyes flickered, frustration already building. "Did Amy call you?"

"About two hours ago. Told me she was staying at your cabin and gave me the number. 'Course, I already had it. Guess you want to know why I didn't tell you about my friendship with her and Vivian."

"You'd be right." Del leaned forward, his eyes boring into Kull. "Why didn't you tell me how close you were to them?" He took off his hat, running a hand through his hair. "Geez, Kull. What were you thinking keeping it from me? You had to know I'd find out."

"I figured as much. Truthfully, kid, it wasn't my story to tell. You needed to learn about Amy's life the last few years from her, not me."

Del mumbled a curse. "I could've arrested her, given her directly to Zoeller to handle."

Kull snorted in disbelief. "But you didn't, did you?"

Looking away, Del thought back over the last twenty-four hours, knowing he wouldn't change anything he'd done. "Fine. So you're like an uncle to her. What do you know about Vivian's death that you haven't told Amy?"

Kull pushed his chair back. Standing, he walked toward Del, leaning a hip against the edge of his desk. "All I've got are rumors, and I wasn't going to fill Amy's mind with stuff I wasn't sure about."

Del stood, meeting him eye to eye. "Then tell me."

An hour later, Del sat in his car outside the cabin, replaying all Kull had told him. The scenario the older man painted might be based on rumors and conjecture, but like Amy's story, it included too much truth to be ignored. And it made sense.

Kull had names, dates, and third party accounts given to him over too many beers in biker bars between Montana and Idaho. Nothing Rick could show to a district attorney in either state, but enough to give the detective several more leads to follow.

Unless given the right incentive, Kull doubted any of the people who talked to him would spill their soul to a cop. It would be up to Rick, and possibly Del, to identify the right type of motivation.

When asked about his plans to head north with his ex-military buddies, Kull shrugged. Before Del left, he'd extracted a promise from Kull to speak with Zoeller. Overall, it had been a good meeting, even with their rough start.

Climbing out of the car, his pulse quickened, noticing the dark interior of the cabin for the first time. Chastising himself for not calling earlier to make sure Amy was all right, he jammed the key into the lock, shoving the door open.

"Amy?" He flipped on the light to see an empty living room and kitchen. He ignored the intense unease when he saw nothing but darkness from the back of the house. Resting his hand on the handle of his gun, he walked down the hall.

Drawing it from its holster, he held the gun in front of him, kicking open the door to the bathroom. After a quick scan, he moved to the guest room. Again, he saw nothing. One room remained.

The knot in his gut moved to his throat, making it hard to breathe. Standing outside his bedroom, he slowly pushed the door open until it hit the wall, then scanned the room. Moving forward, his gaze caught on a slight form hidden under the covers of his bed.

Not lowering the weapon, he edged closer until his legs touched the mattress, a sigh of relief escaping at the sight of blonde hair spread across his pillow. A soft moan, followed by a mumbled phrase, had him setting the gun on the bedside table. Reaching down, his fingers gripped the spread, drawing it down enough to see bare shoulders. Another few inches revealed a bath towel, still somewhat damp, wrapped around her sleeping form. Dropping the covers, he turned away.

Del knew what he should do—grab what he needed and retreat to the guest room for the night. Instead, he unbuttoned his shirt and tossed it over a chair, leaving on the t-shirt underneath. His belt came next, then his shoes, socks, and pants. Rummaging around in a drawer, he pulled out a pair of flannel sleep pants he wore around the cabin on lazy days when he had nowhere to go.

After a quick detour to the bathroom, he drew back the covers on the other side, climbing underneath. Not moving to hold her, he placed his hands behind his head, staring up at the ceiling. It had been an interesting couple days. After years of not seeing or hearing from Amy, here she was, in his bed, and he couldn't do a thing about it. Closing his eyes, he took deep breaths, willing his mind and body to relax.

The feather-soft touch of something on his chest woke him. Before he had a chance to clear his head, a soft moan, followed by a hand on his chest and a weight on his shoulder, jolted him awake. Amy lay sprawled across him, one leg over his, her breathing calm and even.

Instinctively, his arm came around her, holding Amy to him, his other hand stroking her hair. He'd dreamed of this many times over the years, hoping it would happen, knowing the odds weren't with him.

Another soft moan escaped as she shifted against him, his clothes forming a thin, unwelcome barrier. Closing his eyes, Del sucked in a slow, deep breath, blowing it out in a slender stream. He'd just drifted off again when her fingers brushed across his jaw, over his chin, then down his neck.

"Del?"

His body stilled at the whispered word. He shouldn't answer, should pretend to be asleep.

"Hmmm?"

"You're awake."

The deep rumble of his chest as he chuckled provided the answer. She snuggled closer, causing his amused tone to turn into a groan.

"Amy?"

"Hmmm?"

"You need to lie still."

Her answer was to rub against him, her leg brushing up and down his.

"I'm serious, sweetheart." It came out as a plea.

Her amused snicker provided him no satisfaction. "Am I bothering you?"

Before he thought it through, Del flipped her under him, staring down into wide eyes. "Is this what you wanted?"

She didn't answer for a moment, her breath coming in ragged gasps before her lips parted. "Yes." Her arms wrapped around his back, her hands moving under his shirt to feel his taut muscles tighten. "Is this what *you* want?"

He felt the battle slip away. Watching her eyes darken, her tongue darting out to moisten her lips, he lowered his head to within an inch of hers.

"Yes, but only if you're sure."

A nod, the tightening of her arms around his back, was her answer.

Closing the distance, he gave up the fight, capturing her mouth with his.

The sound of his phone woke Del out of the deepest sleep he had in months. The warm weight against his body, slender arm across his chest, had his body heating again. Ignoring the phone, he ran a hand over her hair, kissed her forehead, then groaned when the phone sounded again.

Slipping out from under her, he grabbed his pants, fumbling in the pocket before his fingers grasped the phone.

"Yeah?"

"Where are you? It's almost eight."

Boone's angry voice had Del straightening. He'd forgotten about meeting his brothers at the ranch.

"Uh...something came up. I'm on my way."

"Well, get moving. Thorn and Grace have been here almost an hour. We're wasting daylight."

Cursing under his breath, he tossed the phone onto the bed, rubbing Amy's back. "Sweetheart, you have to get dressed. We need to be on the road in ten minutes."

Her eyes flew open. "Road? What road?" She glanced around, getting her bearings.

Grabbing jeans from a drawer, he slipped into them, then into a clean t-shirt. "We're heading out to the ranch, and we're already late."

Shaking her head, she fumbled with the covers, trying to extricate herself.

Watching, his eyes glinted with amusement, mouth curling into a grin. Walking to the bed, he wrapped his arms around her, lowering his mouth to hers. It was meant to be quick, just a taste. Instead, she wrapped her arms around him, deepening the kiss, wanting more.

Pulling back, he cupped her face. "Keep that thought in mind, sweetheart. For now, we have to get going." Placing one more kiss on her lips, he helped her out of bed, chuckling when she dashed for the bathroom.

A minute later, she ran into the guest bedroom. By the time he'd buttoned his chambray shirt and pulled on his boots, she reappeared, fully clothed, hair in a ponytail. His jaw dropped.

"What? Haven't you ever seen a woman get dressed in a hurry?"

"Honestly...no."

Crossing her arms, she smirked. "Well, I guess I've set a new standard for you."

That wasn't the only standard she'd set, but they didn't have time for that conversation now. Grabbing her hand, he led her into the kitchen.

"Here." He handed her the last two bananas, grabbing two bottles of water from the refrigerator. "Boone will have coffee and plenty of other food at the ranch."

Her features stilled. "Are you sure you want to take me with you? I mean, I'm pretty sure they'll know what went on last night."

Walking up to her, he lifted a strand of hair, rolling it between his fingers before slipping it behind her ear. "They'll guess, but they won't *know* unless we tell them. Boone and Thorn can be gentlemen when they want to be. This morning, they'll want to be gentlemen. Besides, Grace will be there. She won't let either one of them get out of line." Kissing the tip of her nose, he grabbed her hand, picking up his keys on the way to the door. "And you'll get a chance to ride. How long since you've been on a horse?"

She stopped, shaking her head. "I've never been on a horse, Del."

He stared at her. "Never? As in not one time?"

"Not once."

His entire face lit up when he smiled. "Well, sweetheart, you're with the right man. This is going to be a day to remember."

Del was true to his word. Boone and Thorn, ready to pounce when he pulled to a stop, eased up when he got out of his truck and grasped Amy's hand.

"Thorn, Boone. You remember Amy Peterson."

Thorn stepped forward, extending his hand. "Hi, Amy. It's good to see you again. This is my wife, Grace."

Amy shook his hand, nodding before looking at Grace. "I remember you from high school. As I recall, you and Thorn were dating."

"It's a long story, but yes, we were. After graduation, we both left town, then returned, and now look at us." She spread her arms out, smiling.

Boone moved next to her. "Hi, Amy. Glad you're back in town, although not sure how I feel about you being with this miscreant." He nodded toward Del.

Del squeezed Amy's hand. "Hey. I didn't come here to be insulted."

Thorn dropped an arm over Grace's shoulders. "Now that you're here, it's time to wrap up this party and get to work."

Nodding, Del looked at Boone. "What's first?"

"It's a long list. The hay has to be brought in and stacked. The horses need to be rotated to another pasture. The barn has a couple new leaks. The—"

Del let go of Amy's hand, holding his in the air. "I get the picture."

Grace looked at Amy. "You and I can hang out for a while, get food ready for lunch, then ride out to meet them."

"I, um..." She flicked her eyes at Del, biting her lower lip.

Smiling, he gripped her hand again. "Amy's never ridden. When we break for lunch, I plan to give her a lesson."

Grace's eyes widened for an instant before a grin curved her mouth. "I can give her a lesson this morning." She glanced at Amy. "That is, if you're comfortable with me helping you."

When she hesitated, Del spoke up. "Grace is a great teacher. She used to give lessons for extra money during high school."

"I still give a lesson every once in a while. Boone lets me use Sunshine. She'd be perfect for you, Amy."

Amy glanced down at her jeans and tennis shoes. "I don't have boots."

Grace shook her head. "You won't need them for what we'll do today. If you stick around Del, you'll definitely need to get a pair...or two. Come with me and we'll get Sunshine saddled."

"Hold on a sec, Grace." Del took Amy's elbow, guiding her a few feet away. "Are you okay with this? You don't have to take a lesson today if you don't want to."

Sucking in a breath, she forced a slight smile. "Are you kidding? Grace is offering me a lesson while you're out working. It's perfect." Standing on her toes, she kissed him on the cheek. "Go ahead. I'll be fine."

Wrapping an arm around her waist, he gave her a real kiss, lingering longer than intended. Boone's shout had him dropping his arm and backing away.

"Okay. See you at lunch." Hurrying to catch up to his brothers, Del took one more glance over his shoulder, almost tripping, a broad grin plastered across his face.

"That was good." Grace placed a hand on Amy's shoulder.

"Good?"

"It's obvious you're nervous about getting on a horse, but you didn't let Del see it. That's a good thing. Trust me, I won't let you do anything you aren't ready to handle." Moving her hand to Amy's back, Grace guided her toward the barn. "Sunshine is the sweetest horse. She's about twelve years old, right at fifteen hands, so not too tall for you, with a smooth gait. And she loves working in the arena."

Amy stopped at the sound of loud whoop as Del and Boone rode away atop their horses. "Where's Thorn?"

"He'll take the truck and trailer for moving the hay. All three will unload it in the stackyard. I figure they'll be ready for lunch by then."

Amy's brow crinkled. "Stackyard?"

"It's nothing fancy. A fenced in area about twelve feet high. It's to keep the deer and elk away from the hay." Grace grabbed a lead rope off a hook, walking to a nearby stall. Clipping it to Sunshine's halter, she led the mare into the main area of the barn. "Have you ever groomed a horse?"

Amy stayed several feet away from Sunshine, trying to picture herself on top of the mare. "Never, but I'm sure I can learn."

"I'm sure you can, too. Let me show you what to do." Picking up a bucket filled with combs, brushes, and picks, she set it on the ground in front of Sunshine. "First, I'll clean her hooves." Grace grabbed a pick from the bucket, then straightened. "Never approach or groom a horse from the back. Coming at them from an angle is best. That way, you'll avoid their blind spots in the front and back. And talk to them in a calm voice so the horse knows you're approaching. You'll want to groom them from the sides."

Grace demonstrated as she spoke, approaching Sunshine on the side, running her hand down the mare's leg and squeezing the tendon. "Continue to talk in a calm voice. If she ignores you, lean against her shoulder, then squeeze her leg. You'll need to pick up her hoof, resting it on your thigh while you use the pick to clean out dirt, small stones, and other debris."

Feeling as if she'd stepped into another world, Amy watched, her eyes going wide, her features still as Grace moved from one task to another. She told herself she'd learned to ride a motorcycle at thirteen, knew what to wear, the basics of taking care of a bike. This was no different, except she'd be dealing with a live animal weighing ten times more than her.

Grace finished with all four hooves, setting the last one down. "I'm going to use the hard brush now, then saddle her. When we're finished riding, I'll do a full grooming, using all the tools in the bucket. Next time, you'll be doing this." She smiled. "The difference is, you'll be wearing boots."

Amy let out a relieved breath. "I can live with that."

Grace laughed as she set a blanket on Sunshine's back, then lifted a saddle, laying it across the mare's back. "Trust me. You'll do great."

Chapter Eight

Del hoisted another bale onto the trailer, taking off his hat to swipe an arm across his forehead. "I'm not used to this."

Boone crossed his arms, smirking. "You're welcome to join me any day of the week."

Del sent him a bland look. "Let me know when you need me. You know I'll do whatever I can to help."

Dropping his arms to his sides, Boone nodded, the smirk gone. "Yeah, I know you would. The same as Thorn."

"You going to tell us what's going on with you and Amy?" Thorn settled another bale on the trailer, then took off his gloves, stuffing them into a pocket.

Del leaned against the wheel of the trailer, pulling out a pack of gum. "Anyone?" When Boone and Thorn just stared at him, he unwrapped a piece, sliding it into his mouth.

Boone grabbed the pack out of Del's hand, taking a piece for himself. "You're not going to get out of here without giving us the story, so you might as well answer Thorn." Taking off the foil, he popped the gum into his mouth.

Del shrugged. "Nothing's going on. She's an old friend who asked for my help."

Thorn snorted, grabbing his bottle of water, taking several large gulps. "I hear she's staying at the cabin."

"Yeah? From who?"

"Kull."

Del grimaced, shaking his head, mumbling a curse. "I should've figured." Turning away, he started walking to another bale.

Boone followed him. "Where do you think you're going?"

Del held up a hand. "I'm trying to work, not fulfill my brothers' need for gossip."

"Hold up a minute." Thorn jogged up beside him. "You know Grace is grilling Amy right now. You might as well give us the story."

Blowing out a frustrated breath, Del looked at them. "She's back in town trying to figure out how her mother died. I'm helping her, as is Rick Zoeller."

"Didn't her mom die in a car accident?" Thorn asked.

"From what Amy's pieced together, it may have been intentional."

Boone's brow arched. "Murder?"

"Could be. Zoeller is working on it in between his other cases. He thinks she may be on to something." Dell rubbed the back of his neck. "The arson fire in town was at the house Amy was renting. She's sure it was a warning for her to stop digging."

Boone cocked his head, a grin turning up the corners of his mouth. "So she's under your protection. What an unselfish gesture."

Thorn smacked his brother on the back of the head. "Knock it off, Boone." He looked at Del. "Are you doing okay?"

Del pinched the bridge of his nose, shaking his head. "Yeah, I'm fine." He took a couple steps away, then turned back. "Amy and I are trying to..." *What are we trying to do?* "I guess we're trying to see if something could work out between us."

Thorn didn't respond. For once, neither did Boone.

Del thought of the night before, knowing he'd do whatever it took to keep Amy in his life...and his bed.

"That's it. Now, can we get back to work?"

"You're a natural, Amy. I can't believe you've never ridden before." Grace walked alongside Sunshine as Amy guided her into the barn.

Dismounting, she handed the reins to Grace, a self-satisfied look on her face. "I really enjoyed it. After the initial few minutes, my nerves settled down and I was able to relax. It's easy to see why so many people love to ride." Amy winced, knowing she was gushing, but not really caring. It had been so long since she'd been excited about anything. In the span of less than a week, she'd not only reconnected with Del, but also discovered a love of riding.

"Do you think I could come back next week for another lesson?"

Grace removed the saddle and blanket, replacing the bit and reins with a harness. "Of course. I drive to Missoula for classes on Mondays, Wednesdays, and Fridays. If you're up for it, you can come out Tuesday or Thursday and I can give you a lesson."

Amy's eyes lit up. "Really?" Watching as Grace began to groom Sunshine, she stepped up next to her. "I'd like to help."

Grace looked down at Amy's tennis shoes, then back at her face. "Keep watch on how she moves while you brush her down. She's real gentle, but any animal can spook." Reaching out, Grace handed her the curry comb. "Not too hard and go with the grain of her coat."

Amy's first strokes were tentative, slow. Within a few minutes, she'd gained confidence, completing the task as if she'd been doing it her whole life.

"Now do the same with the hard brush."

When Amy finished with it, Grace handed her the soft brush. "This is the last of it. I'll get her face."

Dampening a sponge, Grace cleaned Sunshine's face, glancing at Amy. "You finished?"

"I am." She set the brush in the bucket, placing her hands on her hips. "It wasn't as hard as I thought it would be."

"It's not hard, just part of what you have to do each time you ride. Sometimes after a long day, it's hard to work up the energy to groom your horse. But it has to be done." Taking out her phone, Grace noticed the time, then shot a look at Amy. "We'd better get to the house and make lunch. Those boys will be back soon, and they'll be hungry."

Amy walked beside Grace, taking a good look around at the well-kept yard, freshly painted house, and comfortable furniture on the porch. "This is where they all grew up?"

"It is. They all worked the ranch growing up. Thorn took off for the army. Del went to college, became a deputy, then was elected sheriff. Boone stayed here, attending college at night and a day or two a week. Now the ranch is his life."

Stepping into the house, her gaze took in the homey feel. "It's so tidy."

Grace laughed. "Boone is neat. More than Thorn, that's for sure."

Going to the kitchen, she pulled out what they needed to make sandwiches. Setting it all on the counter, she and Amy began unwrapping meat and laying out bread. After they'd been at it several minutes, she looked at Amy.

"I hear you're staying at the cabin."

Amy's hands stilled, her features tense. "I am."

"It's a nice place. Quiet and out of the way. I know Del loves it there."

Amy's face softened when she thought of the night before. "Yes, he does."

Grace set down the knife she'd been using to cut fruit. "It's none of my business, so feel free to tell me to shut up, but I've never seen Del look at a woman the way he does you. It's the same way Thorn looks at me, as if I'm the only person around."

Amy brushed a strand of hair off her forehead, feeling her face heat.

"You don't have to say anything. I just wanted to say he's a great guy."

"Who's a great guy?" Thorn walked in, wrapping an arm around Grace and tugging her close for a kiss.

Del hesitated when he saw the flush on Amy's face. "Everything all right?" Moving close, he settled an arm around her shoulders.

Nodding, she smiled. "Everything is fine."

"Good." Leaning down, he kissed her. "What did you end up doing?"

Her eyes brightened as she bobbed up and down on the balls of her feet. "I rode a horse."

Chuckling, he pulled her close, giving her another kiss. "You did, huh?"

"Amy did great, Del. Rode Sunshine as if she'd been born on a horse. Even groomed her afterward. Oh, and she needs a pair of boots by Tuesday."

He looked down at Amy. "Tuesday?"

She grinned. "That's when Grace is giving me another lesson."

Del looked at Grace, mouthing, *Thank you,* before looking back at Amy. "Then I guess we'd better get you a car."

Her face fell. "Oh my gosh. I forgot about my car. It's still at the motel." She saw the surprise on Del's face. "It's just a beater, but it's a car."

"Does it run?" he asked.

"Of course it runs. Well, it mostly does. I'm on a first name basis with my roadside assistance plan."

"We'll pick it up after we leave the ranch." Reaching behind her, Del picked up a slice of cheese, taking a bite.

Grace swatted at him. "Hey, that's for lunch."

"I thought this *was* lunch." He snagged another slice, stifling a laugh when Thorn did the same before Boone walked in and picked up one of the finished sandwiches.

"Hey," Grace and Amy said at the same time.

Boone's brows rose, the sandwich stopping an inch from his mouth. "What?"

Waving her hand in the air, Grace gave up. "Forget it. Go ahead and dig in."

Nuzzling Amy's neck, Del whispered in her ear, making her giggle.

"Hey, Romeo." Boone lifted his sandwich. "You need to concentrate on eating if you're going to be any use with the horses."

Amy placed her hands on Del's chest, shoving lightly. "Go on. I need to finish making these last sandwiches."

Taking a seat next to Thorn, Del dug in, gulping down a full glass of water as Amy approached the table with more sandwiches.

"Sit down and eat." He patted the chair next to him. "Grace, did Amy do well enough to ride out with us this afternoon?"

Amy blanched, shaking her head as she sat down. "I don't know if I'm ready."

Grace took a seat between Thorn and Boone. "I don't see why not. She did great on Sunshine this morning." She looked at Amy, seeing the doubt in her eyes. "It isn't far. They're moving horses from one pasture to another."

Amy felt Del's hand squeeze her thigh, doing her best to ignore it. "Um, sure…if you think I'm ready."

He squeezed her thigh again, feeling her slight tremble. "There's only one way to find out."

Boone looked at Thorn, then Del. "Are you two going to be able to stay long enough to help with the barn roof?"

Thorn nodded. "I'm fine with it. Grace brought her laptop so she can complete an assignment."

Del started to speak before stopping to look at Amy. "Do you mind staying a little longer?" He couldn't remember the last time he had to coordinate his schedule with a woman he was seeing. In a strange way, it felt good.

"I don't mind at all. Grace, do you mind if I check my email from your computer? I submitted my résumé for a couple openings and want to see if I received a response."

"No problem at all. Where did you apply?"

Amy finished the last bite of her sandwich, wiping her hands on a napkin. "Gray Wolf Outfitters. Do you know them?" The table went quiet, all eyes on Grace. Amy's gaze passed by each one, halting on Del. "Is something wrong?"

"Nothing's wrong, Amy," Grace said. "Gray Wolf is owned by my family. My father, Wolf Jackson, is the founder and president. If you tell me what positions you applied for, I'd be happy to call him, put in a good word for you."

Amy shifted in her chair, her eyes showing her discomfort. "Oh, no. I couldn't ask you to do that."

"Why not? You need a job and I might be able to help you. That's what friends do—help each other."

"Grace is right, Amy." Thorn draped an arm over the back of his wife's chair. "You should let her talk to Wolf about you. She worked for the company until right before our wedding, so she knows about every department."

"And it's not far from Del's office. You could ride into town with him." Boone grimaced when Grace kicked him under the table. "What was that for?"

Thorn chuckled. "I believe it's for assuming Del and Amy are living together."

Boone shot a look at Del. "I thought she was staying at the cabin."

Amy nudged Del's shoulder, but he just looked at her, not answering. When he stayed silent, she cleared her throat and tried to explain. "Yes, I'm staying at the cabin."

Boone threw his arms up. "Well, there you go."

"Del also has a house in town, a demanding job, and friends. I don't know where he'll be staying. That's why I need my car. So I don't interfere with his life."

Del's jaw tightened before he tore his gaze away from Amy, confused as to why he felt so irritated at her answer.

He'd made it clear he planned to stay at the cabin with her, and up until now, he thought she felt the same. After last night, he'd been certain they'd moved to the next level. He wanted to hear Amy acknowledge they were in a relationship, that she wanted to be with him. Instead, she'd done the opposite, distancing herself, as if nothing had changed between them.

"What Amy is trying to say is she's still figuring things out right now. When she gets a job, I'm sure she'll work out transportation." Pushing away from the table, Del stood, picking up his empty plate. "We'd best get going."

Amy watched him walk out, confused at his behavior. She continued staring as Thorn and Boone followed him, leaving her and Grace at the table.

"Well, I'd suggest we leave this mess for later and catch up to them." Grace stood, heading for the door. "It won't take long to saddle the horses…" Her voice trailed off when she glanced over her shoulder, seeing Amy still at the table. "Do you still want to go?"

Amy felt torn. A few minutes ago, she wouldn't have hesitated. Del's conduct had her thinking about getting a ride back to the motel to get her car, maybe pick up her clothes at the cabin and find a new place to stay.

"You know, Amy, this is all new to Del…and to you. I heard he dated someone a couple years ago, but Thorn says it wasn't serious. In fact, he doesn't think Del has ever had a serious relationship, one that's lasted more than a few weeks. Don't worry too much about what just happened. The best thing you can do is shake it off, get on the horse, and ride out with us. A couple hours on Sunshine will clear your head.”

“You’re probably right. There’s nothing I can do about whatever is bothering Del, so I might as well enjoy myself.”

Grace smiled. “That’s more like it.”

Chapter Nine

"I appreciate you coming by here on a Saturday, Rick." Kull picked up a glass, tipping it toward the detective. "Beer?"

"Water would be great. Thanks." Taking a seat at the end of the bar, Rick glanced around, spotting a couple acquaintances, Harpur and Sam, deep in a private conversation. "Quiet today."

"Don't let it fool you. Saturdays are the busiest, with the action starting early afternoon." Handing Rick his water, Kull sat next to him, sending a quick look to his day manager to take over.

"This is your party, Kull. You invited me and I came. Tell me what's going on."

"Word has it you're doing a little digging into the death of Vivian Peterson. If so, I may have some information for you."

Rick leaned his arms on the bar, glancing over at Kull. "And you heard this from?"

"The sheriff." He looked around, leaning toward Rick "Del encouraged me to talk to you before I leave town. I may be able to add to what Amy has in her notes."

"I'm good with whatever you can provide."

"Good. Let's go back into my office." Walking past the manager, they made their way to the back. "Ignore the mess. It never gets any better."

Rick chuckled. "No worries. This is how I live."

Opening a file cabinet, Kull pulled out a dog-eared folder, glancing through it before laying it on his desk and leaning over it.

"I never showed Amy any of the photos of the people who had *opinions* about Viv's death. I figured if anything came of her search, I'd hand these over to whoever needed them." Spreading out the pictures, he selected one showing a group of men, pointing to specific faces. "These two men are officers in the northern Idaho chapter of the Savage Wolves. Bear is the vice president, and Trip is the sergeant-at-arms." Switching to another photograph, he pointed to the same men again, then to a third one. "This is Frenchy. He's been the president since about the time Vivian left Pete. I can't tell you why, but there has always been bad blood between Pete and Frenchy. It didn't help when Viv filed for divorce, then moved close to the northern Idaho chapter. Frenchy gave her a job, which didn't sit too well with Pete." Kull glanced at Rick. "At least that's what I've heard from more than one person."

"My understanding is you and Pete are friends. Have been for a long time. Did he ever say anything to you?"

Kull straightened, then sat down. "Once. I rode to his clubhouse in White Basin not too long after Vivian and Amy came to Whiskey Bend. You've got to understand, Pete's not an emotional man, never has been. The only two people who could ever get to him were Vivian and Amy. He's not one to apologize, no matter the circumstances, but I never saw him so messed up as after they left. He'd been in love with her for years, never let himself hookup with the women who hung around the club. I don't know what triggered it, but that one night changed everything for him and his family. Kicked the girl out of the club, but the damage was done and there was no going back. Viv had always been clear—if she ever learned he'd cheated, she and Amy would be gone and never come back. I'm telling you all this for a reason. Pete was as much in love with Vivian the day she died as when he married her."

Rick nodded, contemplating Kull's words. "You don't believe Pete had anything to do with her death?"

"None. I know Amy believes differently, but the girl's wrong. Going after Pete is the wrong direction." Kull stabbed his finger at the group picture of the Idaho chapter. "The answer is with these boys in Idaho."

"Do you have anything more on them, such as real names?"

Kull snorted. "Wish I did, but it shouldn't be too hard for you to find out with your database access. Most have done time. The sheriff up there could probably fill you in on what he knows." He closed the folder, sliding it across the desk. "Take this. I've got another."

Picking it up, Rick stood. "You said you're leaving town. Where you headed?"

"North, on a motorcycle trip with a group of guys I served with in the army." Pulling a card out of a drawer, he handed it to Rick. "In case you have other questions while I'm gone."

Pocketing the card, Rick started for the door, then turned back, his gaze narrowing on Kull.

"Hope you're not planning to go anywhere close to Coeur d'Alene. I wouldn't want anything to interfere in the investigation I'm doing."

Holding up his hands, Kull shook his head, doing his best to control a smirk. "I'd never consider doing anything to hinder your work, Detective."

Rick snorted, shaking his head. "Well, just don't get yourself in any trouble while you're trying *not* to hinder my work. Understand?"

Kull grinned, touching two fingers to his brow in a mock salute. "Loud and clear."

Amy and Grace arrived at the barn to find their horses saddled and the men already gone. Mounting, the women rode at a walk for several minutes before moving into a jog. Amy's heart raced at the slight change, surprised at the sense of exhilaration she felt. She'd expected to be afraid and cautious. Instead, after a few more minutes, she wanted to move Sunshine into a lope.

"Keep your heels down, Amy," Grace said. "This is a good time to practice reining her. Be ready. She'll respond quickly to your command."

Amy did as Grace suggested, reining Sunshine left for a few strides, then right, feeling a little more in control with each passing minute. Glancing up, she saw the men herding a group of horses toward them.

"Rein up, Amy. We'll wait for them here."

Amy followed Grace's order, but as the horses came closer, Sunshine began to dance around.

"Hold the reins like this, Amy, and pull gently down. She'll calm down as soon as they pass by us. We'll follow at the back." Grace waved to Thorn as he rode past.

Del rode on the opposite side of the group of horses. Although the herd wasn't large and he couldn't have been more than fifty feet away, he didn't look up or acknowledge her. Amy told herself he was concentrating on the herd and just hadn't spotted her. A small part of her insisted it wasn't true.

She thought back on their conversation at lunch, wondering what happened to upset him. It seemed as if a wall had gone up, shutting her out. This wasn't what Amy expected when she woke up in his arms a few hours before, feeling a sense of peace that had eluded her for so long.

"Okay, let's go."

Amy nodded, following Grace at the back of the herd, her gaze on Del. He rode with such ease and confidence, as if he'd been born on a horse. In a sense, he had. Each movement flowed into the next, allowing him to control his horse with an unconscious grace she envied.

As they continued toward a pasture closer to the house, Amy thought of the last week and how fast things had moved with Del. Although she'd thought of him often over the years, she hadn't realized the extent of her feelings until she saw him again.

Amy believed she'd never been in love. She didn't know what it felt like to love a man or if she even wanted to. After seeing what it did to her mother, she hadn't been in a hurry to experience it for herself. Then Del had caught up with her when she'd run from the fire. The jolt to her senses had been instantaneous and intense. The kind of earth-shattering moment she'd heard friends describe over the years, but never believed. Now she wasn't so sure.

His behavior at lunch forced her to take a step back. Grace said he hadn't been in any kind of relationship in close to two years, and that one wasn't serious. Like her, Del seemed to have short stretches of dating, then would back away, preferring his single existence to tying himself to one woman. Maybe that was what happened today as he relaxed with his family. Perhaps second thoughts found a home in his mind, causing him to rethink the two of them.

She thought of Pete and her mother. *Pete.* Even though she referred to him as Pete, or her father, to others, she hadn't considered him one in a long time. Pete was how she thought of him now and didn't see how that would ever change.

Falling in love with him, then learning of his betrayal had devastated her mother. The beautiful, vivacious woman who loved life and taught Amy so much retreated into herself, becoming wary of any and all relationships...except her friendship with Kull. He'd been the only bright spot during those bleak years between leaving Pete and her death at too young an age.

Amy didn't want that for herself—falling in love and trusting a man, only to have him destroy it all. She needed to rethink what was happening with Del, the way he'd so easily inserted himself into her life, taken care of her, made love to her. She needed to get away and do it soon before it became too difficult to leave.

"Amy. Over here."

She startled, shifting to locate Grace, wondering how she'd made it all the way to the new pasture without realizing it. Reining to a stop, she waited until Grace rode over to join her.

"I called to you several times. You were totally tuned out."

Catching her bottom lip between her teeth, Amy shook her head. "Sorry."

"Hey, no apology needed. You've got a lot going on and tons of decisions to make. By the way, I meant what I said about talking to my father. He much prefers to hire people who are referred to him."

Amy couldn't afford to turn away any help. "Thanks, Grace. I'd appreciate it if you did mention me to your father. If you give me your email, I'll send you my résumé."

"Excellent. I'm having breakfast with him on Tuesday, the perfect time to present it to him. You can give me your phone number when we get back to the house."

"Are you two ready to head back?" Thorn reined his horse to a stop next to Grace, reaching out to grab her hand.

Amy's heart squeezed at seeing the automatic show of affection. Looking around, she didn't see Del.

"If you're wondering, Del and Boone already rode off. They want to get started on the barn before it gets dark."

Nodding, she let out a breath. "Thanks, Thorn. You must all be exhausted." She didn't want to dwell on why Del had left without even a nod or a wave in her direction.

"Not too bad. It's pretty much the way it is on a ranch. Seems Del and I never really left it behind." Reining his horse around, Thorn rode beside Grace, Amy following.

Riding back, she made a difficult decision. After grooming and putting Sunshine away, she'd call a cab and retrieve her car. By the time Del finished with the barn and realized she'd left, Amy would be at the cabin, waiting for him to return so she could get her things. She didn't believe it would be hard to find a place to stay in one of the motels in Whiskey Bend, no longer having the need to hide miles from town.

When they reached the barn, it took only a few minutes for Amy to know she'd made the right decision. Del didn't look down from his spot in the loft, even though Boone, standing next to her, called out to him, saying how impressed he was with her riding. She stared at Del for a long moment, waiting for a smile, wave, or brief word. Instead, he continued to work. Her heart sank, but she told herself it was for the best. Better to move out now rather than stay, wondering when he'd ask her to leave.

Del climbed down from the loft, looking up at the repairs they'd made to the roof. He needed to get inside, pull Amy aside, and apologize. The way he walked out after lunch, didn't acknowledge her when she rode out with Grace, was a jerk move. They needed to talk, clarify what each of them felt before making some other stupid move. If she wasn't as into him as he thought, so be it. She could still stay at the cabin while he'd stay in town. It wasn't what he wanted, but he'd do it if it made Amy happy.

Knocking the dirt off his boots, he stepped into the mudroom, seeing Grace in the kitchen. "Where's Amy?"

When she turned toward him, he paused at the glare she shot his way. "Gone."

Not bothering to remove his boots, he walked toward her. "Gone? Gone where?"

Grace let out a deep sigh, leaning a hip against the counter. "She wanted to get her car. I offered to take her, but she wouldn't hear of it. She called a cab." Her gaze softened. "I'm sorry. I tried, but couldn't get her to stay and talk to you before she left."

Taking off his hat, he ran a hand through his hair, then scrubbed his face. "It's my fault." He slumped into a chair, laying his hat down.

"Yeah, it was."

"I guess she plans to get the car and meet me at the cabin." At least he hoped that was what she had planned.

"She didn't say exactly, but she did ask about one of the motels in town."

"Oh, hell no." Jumping to his feet, Del grabbed his hat, kissing Grace on the cheek as he rushed past her. "Thanks. I owe you."

He didn't slow down when Thorn and Boone called out to him. Raising a hand, he waved, got into the truck, and took off for the cabin. She couldn't have been gone more than half an hour, and she didn't have a key to the cabin to get her belongings. Amy would have to wait, face him, and stay until they talked it out. That was what he told himself over and over as he accelerated to just over the speed limit, wishing he'd handled his insecurities in an entirely different way.

Amy breathed a sigh of relief when she spotted her car in the motel lot, all tires still inflated and no broken glass. Paying the cab fare, she got into the driver's seat, praying as she put the key into the ignition. To her shock, it started right up. If only the rest of the day would be this easy.

She had no intention of leaving her things at Del's, even if she didn't look forward to seeing him right now. Amy had no doubt what happened at lunch was a stupid misunderstanding. Maybe they both overreacted. Del by ignoring her, and Amy by taking off without forcing him to talk about it.

Still, she thought the best remedy was space. Getting a motel room, then an apartment when she found a job would give them both time to figure out if what they started was worth continuing. And Amy needed to decide if allowing herself to fall in love was worth the risk of it all blowing up in the future, as it had for her mother.

Taking the highway, she turned onto the dirt road to the cabin, slowing when she saw Del's truck. Stopping next to it, she forced herself to take a couple slow breaths, reminding herself of the decision she'd made to leave.

Getting out, she took a few steps before spotting Del leaning against a post on the porch, arms crossed, cowboy hat pulled low on his forehead. She sucked in a breath at the sight of him. Without a doubt, he was the most handsome man she'd ever known. It wasn't just his good looks, which, like his brothers, were considerable. Despite what happened today, Del was a good man with a big heart. She'd seen the way people responded to him. They genuinely liked, trusted, and respected him. He'd turned into everything she expected when they'd been friends in high school.

Moving forward, she stepped onto the porch to face him. Before she had a chance to say anything, he reached out, grabbed her arm, and hauled her against his chest, crushing his mouth to hers in the most heated kiss she'd ever experienced. His hands moved up and down her back, pressing her to him, the warmth of his body seeping through her clothes. Dropping her purse, she wrapped her arms around his neck, moaning when the kiss deepened, sending her passion to a whole new level.

Without breaking contact, he reached down, lifting her into his arms. Kicking the front door open, he didn't hesitate, his boots sounding on the wooden floor as he headed straight for the bedroom.

Setting her down next to the bed, his hands moved under her shirt, feeling her fevered skin. He groaned when she unbuttoned his shirt, slipping her hands inside.

Trailing kisses along her jaw and down the slim column of her neck, he settled his mouth on the hollow of her throat, feeling her tremble. His body responded in kind, his hands shaking as he pulled her top off, tossing it aside. Leaning down, he kissed the tender spot below her ear before lifting her again, settling her in the middle of the bed, stretching out next to her.

Looking into her eyes, he slipped a strand of hair behind her ear before kissing her again. "I'm sorry, baby. What can I do to make it up to you?"

Moisture glistened in her eyes, a small smile curving her mouth. "Make love to me, Del."

Those words were all the encouragement he needed.

Chapter Ten

A cool breeze touched Del's cheek, his eyes opening to slits. Too groggy to think, a few uneasy seconds passed as he lay still, trying to figure out what had changed. Then a soft sigh, the weight of her head resting on his chest, her leg crossed over his thigh, settled his mind.

Amy, in his bed, lying next to him. An incredible peace, like nothing he'd ever known, wrapped around him. Glancing down, he lifted a hand, stroking a path along her face, continuing down her neck. His breath caught when she lifted her head, clear eyes locking on his.

"Is it morning?" Her words were slurred from sleep.

Leaning down, he kissed her, continuing to stroke her face with the back of his hand. "Not yet."

Snuggling closer, she closed her eyes, resting her head under his chin, inhaling the scent so unique to Del. She could hear his heart beat as his soft breath washed across her face. The realization she'd never spent the night with a man hit her. Until now, it hadn't been anything she wanted.

Closing her eyes, she tried to get back to sleep. Without thought, she moved the palm of her hand over his chest, enjoying the taut muscles and smattering of crisp hair tickling her fingers. She gasped when Del's hand encircled her wrist, a low chuckle rumbling in his chest.

"I'll never get back to sleep if you keep doing that."

Her lips quivered when she thought of what they could be doing instead of sleeping. "Is that what you want?"

"Sleep? I wouldn't mind a couple more hours." He let go of her wrist, his hand caressing her back.

"When do you need to leave for the office?"

He hesitated a moment. "Seven or eight is normal. Today's Sunday, so unless I get a call, I'm not going anywhere near the office."

She rubbed his chest with her palm once more, enjoying his quick intake of breath. "So does that mean we have time to do *other* things besides sleep?"

His body vibrated when he let out a peal of laughter. "Amy, darlin', are you trying to kill me?"

Raising up on her elbow, she looked down at him, her mouth tilting up at the corners. "Have I worn you out already? I've heard the Macklin brothers have great stamina. At least I've heard it about Thorn and Boone." Before Amy had a chance to enjoy her jab, Del flipped them over, pinning her to the mattress.

Leaning down, he kissed the tip of her nose, the corners of his eyes crinkling in amusement. "And just who are these *sources*?"

A soft giggle escaped when his lips touched the sensitive skin on her neck. "It wouldn't be right to snitch on my informants, Sheriff."

His brow rose. "No? Then you leave me no choice. I'll have to force the information out of you." Grabbing both wrists in one hand, he pulled them above her head, sucking lightly on the hollow of her neck, his other hand roaming down her body.

Squealing with laughter, she squirmed beneath him in a half-hearted attempt to break free. Her laughter faded when his brand of torture intensified, causing a soft moan to escape. Drawing in a ragged breath, she stilled when his mouth continued lower, heat rushing through her body.

"Del..."

"Hmmm?"

"Del..."

This time, he understood her unasked question. "I have you, sweetheart. We've got nothing but time, and I plan to use all of it."

They sat at the table, Amy wearing nothing except his soft chambray shirt, Del clad only in a well-worn pair of jeans. Although starving, she had a hard time concentrating on the scrambled eggs and toast he'd made, favoring the view of the man across from her. A rush of heat flooded her face, thinking of the many times they'd made love last night, already wanting more.

She'd never thought of herself as a sexual woman. Sex had been more a means of escape than a source of pleasure. This morning, she saw it in a whole new light.

"You're staring." Del stabbed a piece of ham, finding it hard to control a grin.

The comment had her lifting her gaze to meet his, refusing to feel embarrassed. "Am not."

Chuckling, he scooped up another forkful of eggs, taking his time to deposit them into his mouth. Chewing slowly, his gaze narrowed on hers. Swallowing, he chased them down with a gulp of coffee.

"You are such a bad liar, Amy. You're either going to have to stop it altogether or learn how to do it correctly. Be warned, my preference is the first one."

Her eyes danced with amusement. "I'll take that under advisement."

Shaking his head, Del pushed away from the table, picking up his plate. "How did your car run when you drove it from the motel?"

Finishing her last bite, she grabbed her empty plate and followed him into the kitchen. "About the same as always. Started fine, which is somewhat unusual. I can't tell you why, but I'm always sensing the car is right on the edge of imploding."

He walked to the front window, opening the wooden blinds so he could look at her car. "Looks to be at least twelve years old."

"Almost sixteen. I bought it in Idaho a couple years ago. Didn't look like much even then, but she was in my budget. I do my best to take care of her. You know, oil changes, checking the tires and fluids. When I get a job, I'll probably look for a newer car." The thought of a job had her walking to the case on the floor, pulling out her computer. "Grace asked me to send her my résumé. She's going to talk to her father about me."

Leaning against the counter, he crossed his arms. "That's a good sign. I'll bet you'll have a job by the end of this week."

Tapping a few keys, she glanced up from the screen, smiling. "You think so?"

"Wolf, Grace's father, will do about anything for her. They've had their ups and downs, but things seem to have smoothed out between them since she married Thorn." He paused for a moment, studying her face. "Are you certain you're ready to settle down in Whiskey Bend and get a job?"

Her fingers stilled over the keys, her head slowly lifting. "Would you rather I not?"

Pushing away from the counter, he held up his hands. "Don't read anything into my question. If it were up to me, you'd get a job and move into my cabin permanently...with me, of course. I just don't want you to feel any pressure to make a decision."

Nodding, she completed her task, then closed the laptop. Leaning back in the chair, she struggled with what she wanted to say, deciding it best to get to the point.

"I've never been in a solid relationship. From what I've heard, you haven't either, at least not for a long time."

His gaze narrowed. "What are you trying to say, Amy?"

She waved her hand in the air. "Doesn't matter. I'm just saying it may be too soon to move in together."

He pulled out a chair, sitting next to her. "What do you want to do?"

Reaching over, she grabbed his hand. "I love the cabin and being with you. It's just, well…with everything going on, I think we may have slipped into this a little fast."

He glanced at their joined hands, then at her, his features unreadable. "*This*?"

Shifting in her chair, Amy cocked her head to one side. "Us, being together. It's moving fast."

Pulling his hand from hers, Del stood, pacing to the window, his back to her. "Too fast for you maybe, but it's not too fast for me. I've been waiting for you to return since we were in high school."

Her chest tightened, hearing the mixture of determination and longing in his voice. "It's not that I don't want to be with you, Del. I do."

Letting out a breath, he looked down at the floor, shaking his head. "I don't want to push you into anything you're not ready for, so I'll ask again. What do you want?"

Standing, she stepped next to him, running her hand down his back. "Time to adjust. I need to make sure what I feel for you is real, and not my emotions playing tricks on me."

Turning to face her, his jaw tensed. He'd become adept at seeing the truth in someone's eyes, hearing it in their voice. Amy hadn't told him everything.

"I know there's more. What is the real reason you want to back away from what's happening?"

Placing fisted hands on her hips, she glared at him. "I am not backing away. I just need to figure some stuff out."

"Like what? I'm a simple man who doesn't go for a lot of drama and rationalizations. Tell me straight out what's bothering you so we can deal with it. It won't get any better if you let it continue to float around in your head."

She felt a ball of dread settle in her stomach. He wanted honesty, to hear what held her back from going forward with what she knew they both wanted.

Shifting so he leaned his back against the window, he rested his hands on the sill and waited.

Opening her mouth to respond, she shook her head, sealing her lips in a thin line. When she started to walk away, Del grabbed her arm, turning her to face him.

"You know what's bothering you. Share it with me. Please."

Forcing away the ache in her chest, she met his intense gaze. "Do you love me?"

"Yes."

The one word, said with such finality, rocked her. Without knowing what it was at the time, she'd fallen in love with him in high school. Why couldn't she join Del in his determination to make this work?

His face softened. "You look surprised."

Licking her lips, she nodded. "I guess I am. At least a little."

Running a hand through his hair, Del asked the question burning in his gut. "Do you love me?"

"Yes."

Closing his eyes, he reached out, wrapping her in his arms. Exhaling a pent-up breath, he leaned down to whisper in her ear. "Then what is holding you back?"

She couldn't look at him as she said the words. "Trust. I don't know if I can trust you."

The shock of her words hit him so hard, his arms dropped from around her and he stepped away.

Lifting her head, she winced, seeing his eyes filled with hurt and confusion. Reaching out, her hand stilled when he moved farther away from her.

"I see." The rough edge to his voice cut through her. "I don't know what more I can do at this point, Amy. I'm here for you. I've always been here for you." Shredding fingers through his hair, he paced a few feet away, then turned to face her. "You may be right. Some distance may be exactly what we both need." Turning, he walked down the hall into his bedroom. A few minutes later, he returned with a small bag in his hand.

Her face paled at the look on his face. "What are you doing?"

"Giving you what you seem to need. There's no reason for you to pay for an apartment when the cabin is available. After you get a job, figure out what you want, then you can make a decision about where to live. If you need anything, you know how to reach me." Leaning down, he kissed her cheek, then walked to the door. Resting his hand on the knob, he hesitated. "I love you, Amy, and I'm not giving up on us, but I want you to be all in. If you don't trust me, well..." Shifting, he glanced over his shoulder. "I'm not your father. I'd never do what he did to your mother...and to you." Without another word, he walked out, shutting the door on a quiet click.

Amy's heart pounded in a painful beat as she ran to the door, pulling it open. "Del, wait..."

Tossing his bag into the back seat of his car, he looked at her, shaking his head. "You wanted time. Well, I'm giving it to you."

Placing a hand on her chest, she rubbed it in a futile effort to stop the pain. Her eyes filled with tears as he drove off, dust rising behind the tires.

Amy didn't know how long she stood there, her mind willing him to come back. Finally, when she accepted he'd left, she gave up and went inside. Plopping down on the sofa, she leaned forward, burying her face in her hands. He'd given her exactly what she'd asked. The knowledge didn't make her feel one bit better.

Gripping the steering wheel so tight his knuckles whitened, Del drove to his house in town. He didn't wait to figure out what to do next. Stomping into the house, he tossed the bag onto his bed, changed clothes, then grabbed the keys to his truck.

Boone always needed help at the ranch, accepting one day a week was about all Del and Thorn could handle. Today, Del would surprise him. Hard, physical work always seemed to calm his mind, helping to push whatever bothered him aside and clear his head.

When done, he'd still be facing an evening without Amy, but at least he wouldn't have spent his day feeling sorry for himself or blaming her. In truth, a part of him understood the issues she had with trust. Pete had really done a number on Vivian and his daughter.

In the blink of an eye, what seemed a strong marriage had shattered, leaving a broken-hearted child. He'd never pushed the issue in high school, avoiding personal questions about her family. They'd kept their conversations centered on school, what they liked to do, and what they wanted to be in the future. They'd stayed after school more than once, wandering into Mike Weiker's classroom. He had a talent for bringing out the best in kids. He didn't pry, mostly listened, but when he did speak, the kids paid attention.

Driving to the ranch, Del found himself wishing Mike was still around. He needed wisdom, and as much as he loved Boone, his younger brother had never been one to get hung up on relationships. Neither had Del...until now.

Turning onto the long drive leading to the ranch house, he sucked in a deep breath. Today would be a time of hard work, a few beers, and listening to Boone spout off about the lack of single women in Whiskey Bend. A normal day with his brother, which sounded pretty darn good.

"That's it, Tyler. One more good hit and it will be in the ground." Boone stood back, out of the way of the young boy with a hammer in his hand.

Glancing over his shoulder, he smiled at Ty's mother, Jenny, the wheelchair she occupied not hindering her ability to join her son at the ranch. For the hundredth time, Boone cursed the disease that claimed the beautiful single mother at such a young age. Even now, with her sallow skin and sunken eyes, Jenny's smile didn't falter. The doctors gave her a couple more months, at most. A short time to figure out what to do with a five-year-old boy who worshipped her.

"I did it, Uncle Boone." Tyler grasped the hammer as he marched toward his mother. "Did you see me?"

Placing a hand on her chest, which Boone knew meant Jenny struggled to breathe, she nodded. "I did, Ty. You're a superstar."

"Did you hear that, Uncle Boone? Mom says I'm a superstar."

Settling a hand on Tyler's shoulder, Boone nodded. "And she's right, little man. Now, do you want to help me in the barn?"

Tyler jumped up and down, nodding. "Come with us, Mom."

Jenny glanced at Boone, sending him a look that conveyed she needed to stay behind. "How about we let your mother rest a bit, Ty. Us men will take care of the work today."

Tyler glanced between Jenny and Boone, not sure what to do. Even at five, he was fiercely protective of his mother. Finally, he nodded. "Okay. I'm going with Uncle Boone, Mom."

A weak smile crossed her face as she sucked in a slow breath. "Okay, sweetheart."

The sound of a truck coming up the drive had them all turning. It took a split second for Boone to recognize Del in the driver's seat.

"You stay here, Ty." Jogging up to the truck, Boone mumbled a curse when Del got out. "Didn't expect to see you today."

"I know you always need help." He looked beyond his brother, seeing the small boy and the woman in a wheelchair. "Looks like you may have all you need."

Placing his hands on his hips, Boone glanced behind him, then looked back at Del. "I don't have time to explain right now, but I can always use help. For now, keep it low key and don't read anything into what I'm doing."

"Because you'll explain it all to me later, right?"

Boone rubbed the back of his neck. "Yeah. I guess I will. Come on. I'll introduce you."

Before Boone could do the honors, Del extended his hand to the woman in the chair. "Hi. I'm Del Macklin, one of Boone's brothers."

Taking his hand, Jenny did her best to squeeze, but she knew her grip only illustrated her growing weakness. "Jenny Davis. Over by the barn is my son, Tyler."

Del's brows scrunched together. "Jenny Davis. Didn't you go to high school with us?"

"I'm surprised you remember."

Boone stepped up beside her, resting a hand on her shoulder. "Del remembers a lot of stuff. Most of it useless."

Jenny's face brightened a little. "Oh, I doubt that's true."

Del shook his head. "Naw. I'm afraid Boone's right. My head is full of useless trivia no one cares about, except me. Thought I'd help Boone out today, if you don't mind company."

"Not at all. I believe he and Tyler were just heading to the barn. I'm going to stay out here under the trees for a bit longer."

Squeezing her hand, Boone leaned down. "You call out if you need anything." She responded with a brief nod. Looking at Del, he motioned toward Tyler. "I'll introduce you to Ty, then we'll start working on replacing some of the stall gates in the barn."

"Sounds good." Del looked at Jenny, touching two fingers to the brim of his hat. "Like Boone said, shout out if you need us." Walking beside his brother, Del lowered his voice. "So you know, I'm not leaving until I get the whole story."

Boone shot him a resigned look, nodding. "Never thought you would."

Chapter Eleven

Amy sat in a rocker on the front porch, cradling a cup of tea. She focused her attention on a squirrel darting up and down the many trees surrounding the cabin, regretting what had happened that morning.

After Del left, she'd fallen asleep on the sofa, waking with a start after another of her unsettling dreams. Like the others, she could remember only a few details, the rest fading away to haunt her in the future.

Taking a quick shower, she'd made a trip to the grocery in town, hoping to spot his car along the way. She had no idea where he lived and hadn't thought to ask. It didn't matter. If she needed him, she'd do as he asked and call.

Leaning back in the wooden chair, she sipped her tea, wishing she could take back what had popped out of her mouth without thought. *I don't know if I can trust you.*

Amy chastised herself for saying such a thing to a man she cared so deeply about. A man who put a great deal of importance on honor and integrity. If their roles had been reversed, Del saying the same to her, Amy would've been tempted to leave and never come back. She'd been lucky he hadn't walked out of her life for good.

Her issues with trust weren't Del's burden. They were hers. She could either find a way to push her father's betrayal into the past or continue to be a victim her entire life. It seemed an easy choice and an insurmountable obstacle all at once.

Reaching into her pocket, her fingers wrapped around her phone, hesitating. This time, she didn't pull it out and stare at the screen as she'd done at least half a dozen times already. Before she could slip her hand out, the phone rang, her hopes rising. Hurrying to check the screen, she let out a disappointed breath when Grace's name appeared.

"Hey, Grace."

"Hi, Amy. Hope I didn't catch you at an awkward time."

"Not at all. I'm sitting on the front porch watching a squirrel scurry about."

"Yeah? And what is Del up to?"

Amy slumped a little in the chair. "I don't know. He decided to stay at his house in town for a while." Raising her cup, she took a few more sips.

"Do you want me to ask Thorn to have a talk with him, find out what's going through his head?"

Choking on her tea, Amy sat up, straightening her spine. "Please don't. It's no mystery why he left or whose fault it is. It's definitely mine, but I'm sure you didn't call to hear about the troubles between Del and me."

"Actually, I called with some good news. I gave my father your résumé and he wants to meet with you tomorrow morning."

Jumping out of the chair, Amy stepped to the rail, leaning against it. "That's wonderful news, Grace. Thank you so much."

"You're more than welcome. Is ten o'clock good for you?"

"Definitely. I'll be there whenever he has time."

"Ten it is."

"Did he mention which position he wants to talk to me about?"

"Sorry, Amy, he didn't. All he told me was to have you come in. Oh, and don't dress up. Business casual is the normal attire."

She let out a nervous laugh. "Good news since that's all I have. Anything else I should know?"

"Not really. Just be yourself. And don't be shy about asking him questions. He loves when people do that. Have you had a chance to research the company?"

"I spent a considerable amount of time on the website before sending in my résumé."

"Good. Have a couple questions ready, and be prepared for long answers. He's real proud of the company he's built."

Amy blew out a breath, trying to stay calm. "Thanks again, Grace. I can't tell you how much I appreciate what you've done."

"If you get a job, we'll all go out and celebrate."

Amy thought of Del, wishing he was here to share the news. "Yeah, we'll do that."

"And don't worry about Del. I've seen the way he looks at you. Whatever is going on will work itself out."

She hoped Grace was right. "I'll call and let you know how it goes."

"I'll be waiting to hear. Good luck."

Hanging up, she stared at the phone, debating about whether or not to call Del. She didn't want to pester him, especially after the way they parted. After a few moments of hesitation, she decided to call him after the interview. Maybe she'd have a job and a real reason to celebrate by then.

"All set." Del stood back after helping load Jenny's wheelchair into the back of Boone's truck.

They'd worked a few hours before breaking to eat the lunch Jenny had brought from town. After Tyler finished, he ran outside, letting the adults talk for a few minutes. Del learned Jenny had been diagnosed with a rare heart condition during her pregnancy. She'd gone her entire life not knowing it existed. By the time the doctors found it, the disease had progressed to a point where treatment had minimal effect.

"Thanks for coming by." Boone took off his hat, scratching his head, avoiding Del's intense gaze.

"Come by the house after you take Jenny and Ty home. Have a beer and relax a bit before heading back to the ranch."

"What about Amy? Won't that cut into your time together?"

Del shook his head, rubbing his chin. "No. She's at the cabin. I'll be staying at the house in town for a spell."

Boone studied his brother's face, not liking the pinched expression. "A beer sounds good. Give me an hour. I'll even bring the beer this time." He climbed into the truck, shutting the door.

"Sounds good. Nice seeing you again, Jenny. Take care of your mom, Ty."

"I will," Tyler shouted from the back seat, waving at Del as Boone headed down the drive.

Del watched them drive off, waiting until they were out of sight before getting into his truck. Sliding the key into the ignition, he settled his hands on the steering wheel, wanting to call Amy. He wouldn't.

Her words about not trusting him had plagued Del all day, cutting deeper into his heart each time. He had no idea how to turn around something out of his control. He had never met her father, didn't want to, yet Pete's actions impacted Amy's ability to trust. There had to be a solution. He just didn't know what it was or how to work through it.

He drove toward town, slowing at the turn to his cabin. The hesitation lasted a few seconds before he accelerated, continuing to his house. On a normal Sunday, he'd stop at the store, picking up food for several days. He didn't have the motivation today. Whatever was in the cupboards and refrigerator would have to do until tomorrow.

Winding through the streets, he pulled into the driveway, parking alongside his cruiser. Most days, he had a predictable schedule. Amy's appearance had changed his routine. To keep his sanity, Del knew he had to get back to it.

Boone knocked once, then let himself in, heading to the kitchen. Spotting Del at the sink, he held up the six-pack.

Del did a double take when he read the label. "How'd you manage to get those? I didn't think the stores carried it."

Stashing the bottles in the refrigerator, Boone pulled out two, handing one to Del. "They carry almost no craft beers, and nothing like this." He grinned, removing the cap and taking a long swallow. "I called Kull."

"I thought he took off with his buddies." Del followed Boone's lead, letting the cool liquid slide down his throat.

"He did. Doesn't mean he doesn't answer his phone or call his manager."

Del smirked. "Hungry?"

Boone shook his head. "Not really. The beer is good for now."

Motioning with the bottle for Boone to follow, Del walked into the living room, settling into his favorite chair. "I'm guessing Jenny is who you've been seeing these last few months."

Boone sat on the sofa, leaning forward so his arms rested on his thighs, the bottle cradled between both hands. "It's not what you think."

Del shook his head. "After meeting her, I'm not thinking anything. Tell me her story."

Taking another sip of his beer, Boone stared out the front window, letting out a slow breath. "You heard most of it from her. Jenny met some guy and got pregnant, but he took off when she told him. I don't think his leaving bothered her all that much at the time. She's an office manager at a law firm and makes good money, or at least she did. She can't work as much as she used to, but the partners have kept her on their payroll. Anyway, her doctor discovered the congenital heart condition during pre-natal exams."

"Don't they usually find out that stuff when you're a baby?"

"Most times. Jenny's birth mom walked out of the hospital a day after her birth...without her. From what Jenny knows, the name and address she used were fake. The state put her up for adoption. Somewhere along the way, the medical records were lost, destroyed." Boone shrugged. "Hell, who knows what happened."

"So she grew up with no clue."

"Her adoptive parents were older, no relatives on either side. By Jenny's account, they were great people. About the time she was twelve, they told her about being adopted."

"Did she try to find her birth parents?"

Boone shook his head, a thin smile turning up his mouth. "She didn't care. Told me her real parents were the couple who raised her." Sitting back, he swallowed another few sips. "Her mother died of cancer her sophomore year of college. Her father died of heart failure a few months after she graduated from school. They left her the house she and Ty live in outside of town."

Del waited, watching a parade of emotions cross his brother's face. He suspected what might be coming next, bracing for the decision he guessed would affect everyone.

"I reconnected with her about a year ago when I went into the office where she works. She was already in a wheelchair. I took her to lunch a few weeks later, learned her story." Boone glanced over at Del. "Except for some friends at the law firm, she has no one. I started stopping by her place a couple times a week. Her condition has worsened a lot over the time I've been around. I've taken her to specialists in Missoula, even went to a doc in Washington who's supposed to be the best."

"And?"

"Everyone says the same thing. Right now, they give her a few weeks, a couple months..." Boone scrubbed a hand down his face.

Del couldn't move, the pain on his brother's face causing his own heart to squeeze. "Do you love her?"

Boone shook his head. "I love the person she is. The way she's fought this thing, never giving up. She still goes to work a couple days a week. That and partial disability keep them in food and clothes."

Del nodded, understanding clear in his features. "I'm guessing you're helping them out."

"I do what I can."

"What will happen to Ty when, well...when she's gone?"

Boone lifted his chin, meeting Del's gaze with determination. "I'm going to adopt him."

His brother snorted, a grim smile on his face. "Figured as much." Draining his bottle of beer, he stood, heading to the kitchen. A minute later, he reappeared with two more bottles. Handing one to Boone, he sat back down. "What can I do to help?"

Standing, Boone walked to the window, staring out into the darkness, taking a long drink of his beer. "When the time comes, be an uncle."

Joining Boone at the window, Del clasped his shoulder. "I can do that. Thorn will, too, and you know you can count on Grace. She loves kids." Dropping his hand, he looked outside. "Have you made the arrangements with Jenny?"

"Yep. It's a done deal."

Del didn't know if he should voice his next question, although it had to be asked. "What about Willow?"

Boone turned toward him, his gaze haunted. "What about her?"

"Come on. We both know she's been in love with you since we were kids. I always thought you'd come to your senses at some point, admit you feel the same for her and marry the girl."

"Marry?" Boone's eyes clouded as he choked the word out. "We both know I'm not marriage material."

Del shook his head. "No. We both know you *weren't* marriage material. I think that's all going to change once you adopt Ty."

Setting his empty bottle on the coffee table, Boone shoved his hands into his pockets. "I care a lot about Willow. Always have. If I were to fall in love and marry, it would be to her, but I lost that opportunity a long time ago."

Del cocked his head to one side. "How do you figure?"

Boone's features twisted in guilt. "A few years ago, she came to the ranch, wanted to talk. You were running for sheriff at the time, and Thorn was still in the army." He paced a few feet away, his back to Del. "We'd, uh...gotten together a couple months before. Actually, we'd been seeing each other for a while when she stopped by." He turned around, haunted eyes locking onto his brother. "She was pregnant."

Del didn't move, waiting for Boone to continue.

"I told her we'd get married. When she asked if I loved her..." His voice trailed off, remembering the day in vivid detail, wishing he'd been a better man. "I told her I didn't, but I'd do what was right. Willow told me she'd rather raise a child without a father than be stuck in a house with a man who didn't care."

Mumbling a curse, Del walked to his chair and sat down. "Why didn't you ever say anything?"

Ignoring the lump in his throat, the pain in his chest, he shook his head. "Pride. Fear. Hell, I don't know. Anyway, she got in her truck and took off. Some drunk sideswiped her on the way back home. She, uh...well...we lost the baby." He choked out the last. "If I'd told her I loved her, she never would've left. She wouldn't have been on the road the same time as that piece of trash who tested way beyond the legal limit."

Rubbing a hand over his head, Del nodded. "I remember the accident. Willow went to the hospital, had a broken arm, bruises, and scrapes. I thought she was pretty lucky. The rest..."

"She kept it to herself. Made sure the hospital said nothing to anyone, including her parents. I still don't think they knew about me and her, or the baby. You've been so busy with your job, I doubt you've noticed, but she barely acknowledges me. It's as if I'm some creature from her past she'd rather forget."

"Don't know how that can be. She owns the feed and tack shop. You must see her a few times each month."

"It took a few visits before I realized she wanted nothing to do with me. One of her clerks always takes my order. Calls when supplies are ready." He snorted. "Guess it's true. You don't know what you have until you've lost it." Walking to the table, he picked up his hat. "Thanks for listening, Del."

Standing, he followed Boone to the door. "Let me know what you need. I'm here for you...and Jenny." He pulled his brother into a hug, slapping his back. "When will you tell Thorn?"

Stepping away, Boone shook his head. "I don't know. Soon, though."

Del watched him leave, Boone's normally straight shoulders slumping as he got into his truck and drove off. Staying by the door, his mind turned to Amy. Right now, the problems they faced seem so small compared to what Boone had shared.

Shaking his head, he closed the door, knowing the term *baby brother* no longer applied to the man who'd driven away.

Chapter Twelve

Amy checked the time again as she buttoned her blouse. Another half an hour before she needed to leave for her appointment with Wolf Jackson.

She'd been on interviews before, obtaining an offer each time. Granted, they were for minimum wage jobs in small companies not close to the caliber of Gray Wolf Outfitters.

Grabbing her brush, she ran long strokes through her blonde hair, letting it curl over her shoulders. She'd toyed with pulling it up, deciding against it. Looking in the mirror, her confidence increased a notch. The light gray slacks and green blouse brought out her emerald eyes. Amy had no idea what to expect, but at least she looked her best.

Checking the time again, she picked up her purse and keys as her phone rang. Her stomach clenched, anticipating it might be Del. They hadn't spoken since he left the morning before, and to say she missed him wouldn't begin to describe the emptiness she felt. Seeing Grace's name, she let out a slow breath.

"Hi, Grace. I'm just walking out the door."

"I won't hold you up. Just wanted to say good luck one more time. I'm sure you'll do great."

"I'll do my best, although I am nervous."

"Don't be. Well, I'd better go. I'm heading into another class. Call me when you're done."

"Will do. And, Grace, thanks again."

Hanging up, she looked around the cabin, her gaze settling on a picture over the mantel of Del with Thorn and Boone. Beside it was one of Del holding up a large trout, a huge grin on his face. Shaking her head, Amy stepped outside, locking the door before climbing into her car.

Turning the key, she froze when nothing happened. She tried a few more times, frustration mounting when she realized the heap of junk wasn't going to cooperate. Pounding her hands on the wheel, she blew out a breath. Getting out, she retrieved her phone to call roadside assistance, tapping her foot on the ground as she waited for them to pick up. When they did, she hurried to explain her situation, her irritation rising at their answer.

"We can have someone out there in about an hour, Miss Peterson."

"An hour! I have a very important appointment in town in forty-five minutes. I need someone here right away."

"I understand and apologize, but this morning's been pretty busy. The two people we have are both already out on calls. Do you still want me to send someone?"

Walking around the car, she leaned her hip against the driver's door. "Yes. As soon as possible, please."

"What's the address?"

She stilled. Amy had no idea. She hated doing it, but she'd have to call Del. "I'll have to call you back. Thanks." Dialing Del's phone, she wished there was someone else who'd be able to help. Kull was out of town on a ride, and her only other option, Grace, was at school in Missoula.

"Good morning, Amy." Del's voice had her heart jumping into her throat.

"Hi..." Her words trailed off as she thought of how to ask for yet another favor from him.

"Are you all right?"

"Yes...I mean, no. I have an interview with Wolf Jackson at ten and my car won't start. I called roadside assistance, but they need an address. If you can give it to me, I won't bother you any longer."

"You aren't bothering me, Amy." She cringed at the exasperation in his voice. "I'll be right there."

"Oh, no. I can't ask you to take time from work to come get me."

"Just stay put. It won't take me long." He hung up before she could respond.

She stared at the car, wanting to scream at the lifeless heap of metal. The last time it wouldn't start, the man who'd come out recommended a new battery. She should've gotten one right away. Instead, she decided to put it off another couple months, or until she got a new job.

Turning back to the house, she walked to the porch, lowering herself onto the edge of the rocking chair. Looking around, she stood, not able to relax. She'd hoped to put off seeing Del until after her interview, maybe be able to give him good news about a job. She just wished something would go right.

Hearing the sound of tires crunching gravel, she hurried to the car, seeing a cruiser come up the drive and stop. When Del got out, he locked his gaze on hers, moving toward her with determined steps. Stopping a few inches away, he placed his hands on her shoulders, leaning down to kiss her lips.

"Good morning," he whispered.

Swallowing, she cleared her throat. "Good morning." The slight amusement on his face had her relaxing.

"Are you meeting Wolf at his office?"

She nodded. "Yes."

"Okay. Hop in. We'll deal with your car later." Grabbing her hand, he walked to the passenger side, opening the door. When she hesitated, he cocked his head. "Is there a problem?"

"Yes. I mean, no." She shook her head. "It's just...I don't want to inconvenience you any more than I already am."

Letting go of her hand, he motioned to the inside of the cruiser. "Get in, Amy. You can call me when your interview is finished, then arrange for roadside assistance to meet us back here."

"If you're sure..."

"I am. Now, get in or you *will* be late for your interview, which you don't want to do with Wolf."

This time, she got right in, strapping on the seat belt. Keeping her hands clenched in her lap, she waited while Del got in, not sure what to make of the way he'd greeted her. It was as if what she'd said, the strain she created, hadn't happened.

Turning the cruiser around, he drove to the highway and headed toward town.

"Did Grace get your résumé to Wolf?"

She looked over at him. "Seems she did."

"Well, if he liked what he saw, he probably has a position in mind. The man doesn't waste time unless he has a plan."

Her brow lifted. "A plan?"

"Yeah. Wolf is the president of Gray Wolf Outfitters, but he's still a detail guy. It would be rare for him to meet with anybody without already knowing what he wanted to achieve. I'm guessing he has a spot you can fill." Del glanced at her. "Which is good. He wouldn't waste his time, or yours."

"Do you know him pretty well?"

Chuckling, Del shook his head. "No one knows him well. Not even Grace. He's a town leader, supported me for sheriff, and works closely with Mayor Barnes."

Biting her lower lip, she drew in an unsteady breath. "Del, about what I said..."

Shaking his head, he held up a hand. "Not now, Amy. You're getting ready for a big meeting. Let's not cloud it with a quick talk about what happened."

"You're right. I should focus on the meeting. We can talk another time."

Pulling to a stop in front of Gray Wolf Outfitters, he left the engine running, turning to face her. "We both need

time to think about what we want. Let's give it a few days,
then we'll talk."

She didn't like the sound of it, but had nothing more
to offer. "Sure. Whatever you want." Opening the door,
she slid out. "Thanks for the ride. I owe you."

Closing the door, she turned, not seeing the stark look
on Del's face. Straightening her back, she walked up the
steps and into the building, determined to make a good
impression. She needed a job. Everything else would have
to wait.

"Then we are agreed, Miss Peterson. You'll start in the
purchasing department tomorrow morning. I'll have my
assistant send you the offer right after lunch. If it all meets
with your approval, sign and send it back. All your
paperwork will be ready when you arrive tomorrow."

Standing, she couldn't stop a broad smile from
crossing her face. Holding out her hand, she clasped
Wolf's. "Thank you, Mr. Jackson. I'm looking forward to
this opportunity." As she placed her hand on the
doorknob, Wolf's voice stopped her.

"You know, I've met your father."

Her hand froze, a chill running down her spine.
Turning, she plastered on a smile. "Oh?"

"You probably didn't know it, but I own the house you and your mother rented while you were in Whiskey Bend. Vivian was a real nice lady. I was sorry to hear about what happened."

Licking her lips, she tilted her head. "How did you meet my father?"

"Pete found out I owned the property and called. Bottom line, he paid cash for the first year's rent, then paid the second year when your mother decided to stay."

Amy's jaw dropped, her eyes widening. "Did my mother know?"

Wolf rested his arms on the desk, leaning forward. "Yes. I refused to accept his money until Vivian knew about the arrangement."

Looking at the floor, Amy nodded. "I see. Well, thank you for telling me." Glancing up, she offered a weak smile. "I'll see you tomorrow morning, Mr. Jackson."

She walked down the hall to the elevator as she thought through what Wolf had told her. She had no idea of the financial arrangement between her mother and Pete, never even considered how she paid rent, food, clothing, and medical bills on her meager income as a waitress. After fending for herself the last few years, Amy now understood her mother could never have done it without help.

Pushing open the front door, she stepped into the sunlight, pulling out her phone. She'd already decided not to call Del. The assistance company probably wouldn't hesitate to pick her up in town and take her to the cabin.

After what Del said, she didn't want to face him right now. And she definitely didn't want to celebrate getting a new job with him.

He requested a few days to decide what he wanted, and she meant to give it to him. Having time away from him didn't sound so good after he'd left Sunday morning. Today, Amy knew she needed space as much as he did, even if her heart squeezed in protest.

It had been a silly notion, thinking something could work out between them. He was the sheriff. She was the daughter of an ex-felon and president of an outlaw motorcycle gang. Even if Amy had distanced herself from her father, she and Del had nothing in common. He'd most likely realized the same and already made his choice.

Waiting a few days to hear it from his lips, staying calm while he rolled out one excuse after another about why they'd never work out, held no appeal. This job offered a new start and she meant to take it.

Tapping the number, she placed the phone to her ear. "Hi. It's Amy Peterson again. Can someone pick me up at Gray Wolf Outfitters?"

Del sat at his desk, trying to concentrate on his work, drumming his fingers as he waited for Amy's call. He'd expected Wolf to take no more than an hour before he made an offer or decided against it, which meant Del should've heard from her at least an hour ago.

He knew she hadn't been happy when he blew off her attempt to talk before the interview. Getting into some heavy discussion of trust and betrayal fifteen minutes before her meeting wouldn't have worked. They needed time to sort out Pete's duplicity and how it affected Amy. He couldn't help thinking he'd made things worse by asking for a few more days. It had been for her benefit, but somehow, he didn't believe she'd taken it that way. The sound of his door opening had Del glancing up.

"Sheriff, Detective Zoeller is out front to see you."

"Have him come on back." Del pushed aside the papers and stood, extending his hand when Rick walked in.

"I hoped to catch you." Rick shook his hand, then sat down.

"Do you have some news on Vivian Peterson's death?"

Chuckling, Rick shook his head. "Not unless you count unofficial, third-party hearsay as news."

Del refused to let his disappointment show. "Hey, anything you learn might be helpful."

"My thought exactly." Rick set a folder on the desk, opening it to one of the photos Kull had given him. "I have a contact in the Coeur d'Alene police department. An old colleague I worked with in California. He got fed up with department politics and decided to make a change several years before I moved here. I sent him some of what Amy supplied and images Kull gave me. Since he wasn't there when Vivian Peterson died, and the accident occurred outside Coeur d'Alene jurisdiction, most of what he told me is what he's heard around the precinct. Department gossip about the police up north."

Del rested his arms on the desk, leaning forward to get a better look. "Savage Wolves MC patches."

Rick pointed to the same three men Kull had mentioned. "Bear, Trip, and Frenchy. He's the president and was the one who hired Vivian when she moved from Whiskey Bend. I don't know if Kull said anything to you, but he doesn't believe Pete was involved in his wife's death."

Del shook his head. "Never said that to me."

"He thinks Amy has been going in the wrong direction because of what happened between her parents."

"Makes sense. It pretty much devastated her and her mother."

Rick nodded. "Turns out Kull's hunch corresponds to what my contact has heard up north. Keep in mind, these are mostly conversations over a weekly poker game that's been going on for years. Savage Wolves is a regular topic for a couple reasons. Trip's brother is on the police force in the small town where the club is located, and the police chief's daughter is the old lady of another member. Both of these add interesting twists on how local law enforcement monitors the club."

"Are you telling me the unofficial policy is hands-off?"

Rick shrugged. "Yes and no. Given the amount of illegal activities the club is into, there does seem to be a lack of arrests and convictions. Regardless, my contact's information leads him to believe these guys have the real story of what happened when Vivian went off the road."

"Has he heard anything about why the car was demolished so soon after the accident?"

Rick pinched the bridge of his nose. "The officer who made the call to pick up and demo the car is Trip's brother. The demo company is owned by..." He looked at Del.

Del shook his head. "You're kidding me."

"Nope. It's one of Savage Wolves' legitimate businesses."

"What about Pete? No one thinks he was involved?"

"Since it was ruled an accident, he was never considered a person of interest. Checking further, it wouldn't have mattered anyway. Turns out, on the day of Vivian's death, Pete and most all of his club were at a rally in southern Montana with the Bozeman and Billings clubs. Not a chance Pete or one of his men could've made it to Idaho, forced her off the road, then made it back to the rally without people noticing."

"Couldn't he have arranged to have it done by the Idaho chapter?"

Rick shook his head. "Too much bad blood between Pete and Frenchy. If Pete wanted it done, he would have gone over with a couple of his brothers, or sent a group to handle it. And there's something else." Del glanced up as

Rick pulled a document out of his pocket. "Look at this." His finger slid down one column, then another. "Pete's been sending Amy money every month since Vivian's death. He also paid for her funeral and all her debts."

Rubbing the back of his neck, Del took one more look at the numbers. "Why would he do all this if he wanted her dead?"

"He wouldn't. Pete still might have sent money to Amy, but the rest...not a chance."

"What's the next step?"

Leaning back in his chair, Rick crossed his arms. "As you know, the case is out of my jurisdiction. Since it was ruled an accident, it isn't in the files as a cold case."

Del saw a hint of determination in Rick's eyes. "What are you suggesting?"

"I've got a few days of vacation available."

His lips tilting up into a smile, Del nodded. "Same here."

Standing, Rick picked up the folder. "Guess it's time for a road trip."

Chapter Thirteen

Amy hadn't answered her phone since returning to the cabin, watching as the mechanic installed a new battery. It set her back a couple hundred dollars, but it was worth every cent if it got her to work on time tomorrow.

After changing clothes and eating a sandwich, she'd called Grace, giving her the good news. At first, Amy had been hesitant to accept an invitation to have dinner with her and Thorn later in the week. Her preference had been to take them out as a thank you for the referral to Wolf. Grace wouldn't hear of it, saying Amy could take them out after she'd banked a few paychecks.

Sitting at the computer, she stared at the screen, debating whether or not to send an email to Del. He'd gone out of his way to pick her up, probably didn't even realize how his decision not to see her for a while had hurt.

When she'd finally checked her phone, there were two voicemails and a text from Del, each inquiring as to how the interview went and if she needed help with the car. His voice gave no indication of being upset, just curious. Somehow, that tugged at her heart even more.

All these years, she'd survived on her own, independent, not allowing anyone to get close. It had all crumbled within a week of reconnecting with Del. Then she'd voiced her worst fear, and the time they'd spent together vanished with the quiet closing of the front door.

When he'd arrived this morning, his greeting had been more than she expected, sparking hope he truly did want to keep seeing her. Now she wasn't as confident.

No one knew her weaknesses as well as Amy. Each time she began to get close to anyone, an invisible wall would form, keeping her safe while warning them off. Bucking the sensation and defeating her fears had never occurred to her until the extent of her feelings for Del had become clear. She loved him.

The realization stunned her at first, then scared her. She'd watched what loving someone had done to the two people who meant the most to her. Amy had learned the hard way how one betrayal could destroy trust, ruining a relationship in less than a heartbeat.

Instead of voicing her fear so they could discuss it openly, she'd thrown it in his face. If she could take the words back, she would.

Shutting the computer, Amy rubbed her temples, wishing her acute need for Del would stop controlling her thoughts. She'd gone years without him. Why couldn't she rid him from her mind now?

Pushing back from the table, she wandered down the hall, entering Del's bedroom...her bedroom until she found an apartment. She refused to take advantage of his hospitality any longer than necessary. Two weeks maximum and she'd be gone.

A tiny voice inside Amy's head reminded her of the money Pete had deposited into her checking account each month. She'd grown so accustomed to living on what her alter ego, Susan Miller, had earned, she'd forgotten about the money lying untouched in the bank. As much as Amy wanted to stay at the cabin, she didn't like the idea of taking advantage of Del longer than needed.

Changing into her sleepwear, she ran a comb through her hair several times before making a decision. Setting the brush down, she rummaged through the drawer where she'd stowed her belongings, pulling out her checkbook—the one in her real name with the money Pete had provided. At lunch tomorrow, she'd open a new account, then start looking for a place to live.

By the time Del was ready to talk, she'd be back on her own, no longer indebted to him. Amy liked the idea…a lot.

"Another hour and we'll reach the outskirts of Coeur d'Alene." Del drove the almost empty highway, enjoying the scenery, as he and Rick talked through what each knew about Vivian's death.

They'd left at five in the morning, Del insisting on taking his truck on the three hour drive. Their first stop would be to meet with Rick's contact, Pierce O'Brien, his former colleague in California. They'd plan the rest of their time in Idaho after talking to him.

Del glanced at Rick. "Tell me about O'Brien."

Rick rubbed his chin, a wry smile crossing his face. "He's a maverick, does things his own way. Unlike others, he's been able to make it work for him."

Del's eyes narrowed. "What do you mean?"

"Pierce is clever and has incredible instincts. He never gives too much away, even as he's picking up all kinds of good information about others. It's what tipped him off that something was off with Vivian Peterson's death. Other cops might make comments, give an opinion, but never do anything further. Pierce listens, and if he thinks the pieces don't fit, he'll continue to dig until he's happy with the answers."

"I take it he isn't happy with what he's learned."

Rick nodded. "Not from what he's said to me. Too many missing pieces and unanswered questions. Plus, he's in Coeur d'Alene, which is south of the town the Savage Wolves call home." He shifted in his seat. "It isn't as if Pierce hasn't run into this type of situation before."

"How so?"

"We have about every flavor of outlaw gang in the area around San Francisco. They each have their own territory, but conflicts arise and the results aren't pretty. One gang in the East Bay had deep ties to local law enforcement. The club vice president's old lady was on the police force, as was her uncle. Her sister, a district attorney, was married to the sergeant-at-arms. Half the police department was on the club's payroll, plus a decent number of deputies."

Del's eyes widened. "The sheriff's department, too?"

"Yeah. It was a spider's web of relationships, payoffs, and favors owed. Pierce landed on a joint task force with orders to shut down club activities. They didn't get far. Made a couple raids, arrested three or four members on weak charges. A total fiasco. He's certain at least one person on the task force was on the gang's payroll, but never had enough evidence to prove it."

Rick looked at his information, pointing to a coffee shop up ahead. "Turn in up there."

Parking, Del got out of his truck, stretching his arms above his head. Hearing his phone, he pulled it out of his pocket, seeing Grace's name. He let it go to voicemail when a large, burly man walked up to Rick, wrapping him in a hug.

"Pierce, this is Sheriff Del Macklin. Del, meet Pierce O'Brien."

Pierce gripped Del's outstretched hand. "Ah, the boyfriend."

"Boyfriend?"

Rick chuckled. "My fault. I told him about you and Amy. Figured he needed to know why this is surfacing now."

Nodding, Del followed the two men into the restaurant several miles south of Coeur d'Alene. The waitress settled them in a large, U-shaped booth near the back, a quiet corner where they could talk without being overheard. Pierce didn't ask before ordering three of the breakfast specials and coffee, flirting with the waitress before she walked away. From that instant on, he was all business.

"First, I want to make sure we're all straight on a few critical details. Mrs. Peterson didn't die in the local jurisdiction. Her crash occurred north of here, in a small town the Savage Wolves call home. We usually don't get involved in cases up there because they have their own police force. They're in a different county, so they also have a separate sheriff's department. Once in a while, we help each other out on cases, provide backup if something big is going down. Other than that, we don't interact much. My chief is a standup guy. From what I've heard, I can't say the same for the chief up north."

Leaning forward, Del narrowed his gaze on Pierce. "I know Amy believes her mother was murdered, and after seeing what she's dug up and the threats against her, I have to agree. What makes *you* so certain her death wasn't an accident?"

Resting his arms on the table, Pierce took a quick glance around. "Even though the two cities have separate forces, the social connections are intertwined. The guys in my department have friends up north. They hunt together, go on fishing trips, have family barbeques. Distance doesn't matter to them. Some of the guys in the force up north transferred there from Coeur d'Alene. I've been on a couple of their hunting trips. We compare notes on what's going on in our towns. Over a few beers, people loosen up, talk more than they should. I listen. After a while, I started hearing a lot of the same about Vivian's death. I never asked questions. Didn't have to. I can't give you anything that would hold up in court, but I can give you enough to talk with people, see if there's a thread you can pull that will unravel this mystery."

Pierce leaned back when the waitress arrived with their food. Ignoring the steaming meal, he continued. "I'm not in a position to inquire further or conduct a formal investigation, so your timing is perfect."

"We don't have much time, Pierce. Del and I only have a couple days up here, so we have to connect with the right people." Rick lifted his fork, taking a bite of his breakfast.

Reaching into his pocket, Pierce pulled out a folded piece of paper, sliding it across the table to Rick. "A list of who to talk to, why they're important, and where to find them."

Unfolding the paper, Rick whistled. "This isn't a list. It's a full report on what you've found. You've done a lot of our work for us."

Pierce shrugged, chewing a piece of bacon, washing it down with a sip of coffee. "After working on the task force in the Bay Area, I found life in Idaho a little tame. When I heard the guys talking about Vivian's death, I decided to dig a little deeper. I'm divorced. No kids. It's a better way to spend my time than sitting in a bar tossing back whiskey."

Handing the paper to Del, Rick pulled out his wallet, tossing more than enough money on the table to cover all three meals. "We'd better get moving if we're going to get through the list. I'll call you later today so we can meet up for dinner."

Standing, Pierce nodded toward the list Del held. "Most of those places are bars up north where the bikers hang out. It'll take you about an hour to get there from here. Watch your backs. That region is pretty much controlled by the Savage Wolves."

By five o'clock, they'd already hit four places on Pierce's list, talked to half a dozen people, including four bartenders. They'd learned nothing new, except most thought it a freak accident. One figured Vivian had dropped her cell phone, leaned down to retrieve it, and went off the road. Another figured she'd fallen asleep at the wheel.

"Let's hit one more place before I call Pierce." Rick studied the list, selecting one heading toward Coeur d'Alene. "Looks to be about four miles south of here."

Del slapped the wheel with his hands. "Somebody's got to know something."

Rick rested his head against the seat. "No doubt somebody does. We just haven't found them yet."

"I don't know why I thought coming up here would be the key to unlocking the mystery."

Chuckling, Rick glanced at him. "You're an optimist at heart, Del. That'll change the longer you're sheriff."

"Perhaps." Del didn't like to consider his perspective would change the longer he stayed in law enforcement. "You seem to have stayed pretty balanced."

"It's a façade. I was a real optimist when I started. The harder I tried to look for the goodness in people, the faster my outlook changed. Comes with dealing with people who cheat any chance they get and lie with ease. Most don't believe it's wrong to break the law." Sitting up, he pointed to a run-down bar on the right side of the road. "Don't get me wrong. I still believe most people are good. But there are enough bad ones, I find myself trusting fewer people, keeping to myself more than I used to."

Pulling to a stop in the gravel lot, Del cut the engine, looking at Rick. "Well, that's about to change. When we get back, we're going to start meeting regularly for beers at Wicked Waters."

Making their way around several parked motorcycles, Del stopped next to one he'd seen many times. A slow smile tilted the corners of his mouth as he turned to Rick.

"Kull's bike. This must have been as far as they got." Walking inside, his eyes locked on the group of motorcyclists around a table, Kull sitting with his back to the wall.

Rick headed straight to the bar, glancing over his shoulder. "You grab us a couple chairs and I'll get us some beer."

Kull didn't notice Del striding to their table until he stood within a few feet of him. "This as far as you got, old man?"

Looking up, Kull's eyes brightened. "Hey, kid. Didn't expect to see you up this way." Standing, he pulled Del into a hug, then turned to the others. "This is—"

Interrupting, Del stuck out his hand to the man closest to him. "Del. I'm a friend from Whiskey Bend. This man walking up is Rick."

Setting down two glasses, Rick nodded to the group. "Do you mind if we join you?"

"Not at all." The one closest to Del pulled up two chairs.

When Del looked back at Kull, he saw a hint of confusion on his face. A quick shake of his head had his friend's brows drawing together, but Kull didn't ask any questions as he sat back down.

"How long have you been in Coeur d'Alene?" Rick asked, sipping his beer.

Kull spoke for the group. "A couple days. We'll spend a few more before heading back to Whiskey Bend."

From there, the conversation moved in many directions. An hour later, the group decided to head out for dinner. Standing with the others, Kull looked at Del, then back to one of his friends.

"You guys go ahead. I'll meet you at the restaurant."

Watching them shuffle out, he nodded to a smaller table near the hallway leading out back. Taking a seat, Kull pulled the chair close to the table, leaning forward.

"We need to find out about Vivian's car." He sat back when a young man walked up to wipe down their table. When he moved back toward the bar, Kull started again. "The towing company took the car to their wrecking yard. It's owned by the club, but there may be someone who will talk."

The young man reappeared, looking nervous as he glanced about. "More beer?"

Del shook his head. "We're good."

He seemed to hesitate before turning away to head down the hall.

"I was in here last night before the rest of the group showed up. I've met the bartender before." He nodded over his shoulder. "He's been in this area a long time. Seems to know a lot about the Savage Wolves, but refused to say much about Vivian's death."

Del leaned in closer, lowering his voice. "Any indication he thinks it wasn't an accident?"

"I asked him about that. He closed up, wouldn't say another word to me."

Rick watched the bartender as he set some drinks on a tray, signaling for the waitress. "His reaction says more than words. I agree, Kull. Our best bet is the wrecking yard. This may take more than two days, Del."

Looking up, Rick noticed the young man hovering a few feet away, taking a long time to wipe down a table he'd already cleaned a few minutes before. His instincts kicked in when the man saw him watching and hurried back down the hall.

Kull stood, clasping Del on the back. "I need to get going. We'll plan to catch-up back in Whiskey Bend." Nodding to Rick, he took off.

Del looked at Rick. "Let's talk to Pierce at dinner. He might have some ideas."

"We should take off, too. I don't think we'll get any more out of the bartender than Kull did."

Approaching the truck, Del's head swiveled at the sound of a low whistle. "Did you hear that?"

Rick nodded, hearing a low shout.

"Over here." The young man from inside stood near a dumpster behind the bar, motioning them over.

Looking around, seeing no one else outside, Rick walked over to him, Del staying at the car. "You have something to say?"

The young man swallowed, indicating for Rick to follow him around the building.

Rick planted his feet, leaving his arms relaxed at his sides. "Anything you have to say can be said right here."

Wiping sweat from his brow, he nodded. "Okay, but this has to be quick."

"What's your name?"

"Kenton." His gaze darted around, his voice shaky. "Are you looking for information on the Peterson woman?"

Rick stepped closer. "What do you know?"

"I've got what you need, but it will cost you three thousand."

Rick shook his head. "Too much." He began to turn away when the man grabbed his arm.

"Two thousand." He could see Kenton's hand tremble and wondered if he was on meth or if the shakes were due to something else.

Glancing at his arm, Rick removed the man's hand, smirking. "Maybe a thousand. First, give me enough so I know you have something of value."

Clearing his throat, Kenton looked up, his eyes glassy. "I was a prospect with the Wolves. Worked at the wrecking yard when she died."

Eyes narrowing, Rick crossed his arms. "Why turn on the club?"

Hatred flashed through Kenton's eyes before his face hardened. "When it came to a vote to patch me in or not, Bear didn't back me. Spewed some kind of trash to Frenchy and the others. I could've stayed as a prospect, tried to turn it around, but Bear was after me. I took off that night, leaving my cut on the bar, and rode to Washington."

"But you came back."

"A few months ago, my ma took ill, so I came back. Believe me, I wouldn't have, except she needs my help." Kenton met Rick's gaze. "That's all I'm going to say right now."

Rick glanced over his shoulder at Del, then back at Kenton. "Where do you want to meet and when?"

"The Red Raven is about ten miles south of here. Right off the highway. Eleven o'clock tonight."

Before Rick could respond, Kenton turned, rushing to get back inside the bar.

At eleven, Del, Rick, and Pierce sat in the parking lot of the Red Raven, impatient to learn what Kenton had to say. About ten after eleven, a motorcycle pulled up next to them. Kenton got off, climbing into the back seat beside Del.

Kenton looked out the back window. "Drive."

"Where?" Rick sat in the driver's seat of Del's car, glancing in the rearview mirror.

"Doesn't matter. I just don't want to sit here where anyone can see us." He looked at Del. "You got the money?"

"A thousand dollars. You give us what we need and you're welcome to it." Del patted his pocket.

Licking his lips, Kenton blew out a breath before clearing his throat. "What do you want to know?"

Pierce turned from the front passenger seat, pinning Kenton with a hard glare. "All of it. Anything you know about Vivian Peterson's death."

"I was a prospect when she came to work at the club. Nice lady. Everyone liked her, especially Frenchy."

"The president?" Del asked.

Nodding, Kenton continued. "Had it bad for her. Everyone knew it, too. But she was still married to Pete, the president in Montana. Something happened between them and she split a long time before coming to Idaho." Licking his lips again, he glanced back out the window. "Bear, the vice president, didn't like the way Frenchy protected her. Said the prez was losing focus because of a woman. They got into a lot of arguments about her."

"How do you know this?" Pierce asked.

"You learn a lot when you keep your head down, do everything they ask, and become invisible. I was a nothing to them, just someone to do all the dirty work while they pulled off the big jobs. The last argument was a few nights before Vivian died. She came to work at the bar. Sometime after ten, Bear hit on her pretty hard, told the other bartender to take over while he grabbed Vivian, tried to force her down the hall. Frenchy went nuts, shoved Bear against a wall, told Vivian to get out of there. Told me to follow her home. I didn't see the actual fight, but I heard about it, and saw how Frenchy and Bear looked the next day."

Del pulled a bottle of water from a small cooler, offering it to Kenton. Downing half of it, he took another deep breath.

"A few days later, Bear comes to me before lunch. Tells me a car will be towed in late that afternoon. It's to be run through the crusher right away, no questions asked and no talking to anyone else in the club. Not even Frenchy."

Rick looked at Kenton in the rearview mirror. "Did that cause you to hesitate? Maybe think something wasn't right?"

"Hell yeah, it did. But Bear gives the orders at the wrecking yard. Asking questions only resulted in pain, so you learned to follow orders."

"What did you see when the car came in?" Pierce asked.

"About what you'd expect. Blood on the windows, seats, and dash. Funny thing was the car was only smashed in the front where it slammed into a tree. Other than that, it was in pretty good shape. Except for one thing."

Del stared at him. "What was that?"

"A big dent behind the passenger door on the driver's side. She had a white car. The dent had red paint imbedded in it." He looked at Del. "Bear's truck is red."

Chapter Fourteen

Amy woke with a start. She had a hard time sleeping the last two nights, thinking about her new job and wondering where Del had gone. Grace called the day before, asking if Amy had heard from him. She hadn't.

One of the deputies told Thorn he didn't know where the sheriff had gone, except he'd taken a few days off. This prompted Thorn to call Boone. Both tried Del's phone, getting voicemail, leaving an insistent message for him to get in touch with one of them.

Boone tried Kull, knowing he was on a road trip with friends. He hoped to hear back from him soon.

Getting dressed took little time, allowing her a few extra minutes to make coffee and down a bowl of cereal before grabbing her keys. To her relief, the car had started without a hitch the last two mornings. She wished her cell phone worked as well. Del had warned her reception could be sporadic. Until last night, it had been pretty good.

Getting into the car, she checked the screen on her phone, seeing enough bars to call Del. Tapping his number, her heart sped up as she waited. The same as his brothers, her call went to voicemail. She didn't leave a message. Shoulders slumping, she set the phone aside, telling herself they both needed space, even though she'd begun to feel the opposite.

Turning onto the highway, Amy felt a flutter of excitement about another day at her new job. She found the work challenging and stimulating, the people easy to be around. The salary had been more than she expected, enough to afford a one bedroom in the apartment complex down the street. Amy had an appointment with the property manager on Saturday. He'd told her a furnished unit would be available at the end of the month.

Tonight, she'd go to Grace and Thorn's house for dinner in celebration of her new job. Since no one had heard from Del, she felt a pang of disappointment, knowing he wouldn't be there.

Parking in the employee lot, she used her key to access the side entrance, hearing her phone ring. She didn't bother to look at the screen before answering.

"Hello?"

"Amy, it's Del."

Her breath caught as her fingers fumbled with the phone, nearly dropping it at the bottom of the stairs. "Hey. I heard you're out of town."

"I meant to call and let you know."

"It's all right, Del. You don't owe me an explanation."

"I talked to Thorn this morning. Heard you got the job at Gray Wolf. That's great, Amy. Congratulations."

"Thanks. I started in the purchasing department the day after the interview. So far, it's going very well."

"If you don't have plans for lunch, can you meet me at Evie's at noon?"

Amy looked into her purse at the packaged lunch and apple she'd picked up at the grocery. They'd be fine in the refrigerator at work. "I'd like that."

“Great. I’ll see you then. And, Amy?”

“Yes?”

“I’ve missed you.”

Even though work kept her busy, Amy rushed through the stack of order confirmations from suppliers, her excitement building as the clock ticked closer to noon. She hadn’t expected the rush of relief she felt when Del said he had missed her.

“A group of us are going to the sandwich shop next door. Do you want to join us?”

She glanced at the young woman who worked at the desk next to hers. “I’d love to, but I’m already meeting someone at Evie’s. Another time?”

“Sure. A few of us usually go to Doc’s once a week.”

Amy had been to Doc’s Grill and Tavern a couple times since coming back and loved it. Homestyle food with portions big enough to have for lunch or dinner the following day. “Great. Count me in the next time you go.”

Seeing the clock strike noon at the same time the old bank clock chimed outside, she grabbed her purse. Taking the stairs faster than she should, Amy slowed her pace when she stepped outside. She didn’t want to appear too eager to see Del, but didn't want to waste a moment of her short lunch hour, either.

Passing Scorpion Custom Motorcycles, she waved at Thorn standing outside, talking to one of his partners, Josh Reyes. The same age as Thorn, Josh had gotten her attention in high school when she'd seen some of his drawings. Thin and wiry then, he'd grown taller and added a good deal of muscle over the years. She continued to stare as she walked past, hearing a familiar voice behind her.

"Don't tell me you're checking out Josh." Del caught up to her, settling an arm over her shoulders, giving Amy what was meant to be a quick kiss, becoming more with little effort.

"Hey, bro! Get a room."

Breaking the kiss, he glanced behind him, seeing Thorn and Josh laughing. He considered flipping them off, then thought better of it. Del didn't need anyone seeing the sheriff giving someone the finger.

"Tonight. Dinner at our place," Thorn called.

Del nodded, taking Amy's hand. "We'll be there."

She couldn't suppress the heat rushing through her at his passionate greeting, nor the way he gripped her hand as they entered Evie's.

"Anywhere you want," Evie called over the noise when she saw them walk inside.

Leading her to a booth by the window, he surprised Amy by slipping in next to her. "Hope you don't mind being this close to me."

Running her tongue over her lips, she smiled. "Not at all."

"What'll you two have? And, Del—"

He held up his hand, silencing her. "Don't even say it. I'm not going for the ham and cheese on sourdough today, Evie."

Resting her hands on her waist, she tilted her head. "Do tell. And what is the sheriff ordering today?"

He looked at Amy. "You first."

"Club sandwich on sourdough, fries, and an iced tea, please."

Evie nodded at Del, a brow arching.

"A Reuben with fries and an iced tea."

Evie's eyes widened. "Wow. You *are* stepping outside the box, Del. I'll get these going for you."

Reaching under the table, Del picked up Amy's hand, lacing his fingers through hers, his face solemn, his gaze intense. "I have news for you."

Nodding to Evie when she set down their drinks, Amy looked back at Del. "What kind of news?"

Looking around, he lowered his voice. "Rick Zoeller and I took a road trip to Coeur d'Alene." When her brows furrowed, he lifted their joined hands, kissing her knuckles. "I should have called, but it happened fast. We met Kull up there."

"Uncle Kull?"

Taking a sip of tea, he chuckled. "That would be the one. Anyway, we connected with someone who worked at the wrecking yard where they took your mother's car."

As he continued the story, not leaving out any of what Kenton told them, Amy's eyes widened, her grip on his hand tightening. By the time he reached the part where Kenton mentioned Bear's truck being red, she choked out a sob. Letting go of her hand, he placed an arm around her shoulders, pulling her close.

"Are you all right, sweetheart?"

Swiping away a tear, she nodded. "Sorry. I've just always thought..." Her voice trailed off as she rested her head on Del's shoulder.

"It's okay, darlin'. After all that's happened, it's natural you would think Pete had a hand in her death."

She looked up at him. "He didn't, though."

"No. According to Kull, Pete always believed it was an accident."

When Evie returned with their food, Amy drew away, waiting until they were alone. "What now? I imagine Rick is giving the information to the Coeur d'Alene police."

Del's lips formed a thin line. Although he and Rick had discussed what to do at length, they'd done what was expected of two lawmen and met with the police chief. He'd been less than enthusiastic, news Amy didn't need to hear.

"The chief took the information. I don't know what will happen next. He was pretty pissed we didn't come straight to him when we arrived in town."

"But he'll follow-up, right?"

"I'm sure he'll do all he can." The lie came hard. Del didn't believe for an instant the chief would do anything more than file what they gave him in some cabinet. "We met with Kull after leaving the police station. We agreed he'd be the best person to tell Pete what happened. He and his friends rode over there yesterday. We'll know more after they meet."

Amy gripped his arm, her eyes filled with fear. "He can't let Dad retaliate. He will go back to prison if he does something stupid, like go after Bear."

Glancing around the diner, Del leaned toward her. "That's the first time you've called your father Dad."

Blinking a few times, she nodded. "Guess you're right. I suppose I'm feeling guilty for blaming him all these years. When I met with Wolf Jackson, he told me he remembered my mother. He owned the house where Mom and I lived. He also said he knew my dad." She sucked in a shaky breath, more guilt coursing through her. "Wolf told me Dad paid the rent the entire time we lived in Whiskey Bend. He's also been putting money in my checking account every month for years." Burying her face in her hands, she shook her head. "I've been so awful to him, Del."

Reaching up, he pulled her hands away. "Even though his actions tore your family apart, I don't doubt he still loved you and your mother. People do stupid things, sweetheart. Unfortunately, what he did could never be undone."

"Not in the eyes of my mother. No matter how much she still loved him, she could never trust him again. The pain was just too great for her to overcome."

"It's understandable. The question is, will *you* be able to forgive him?"

Returning to his office, planning to pick Amy up at the cabin after work, Del sat down, breathing a sigh of relief. He hadn't wanted to discuss what Pete might do with the information on Bear. He and Rick had done their job, reported all they knew to the police in Idaho. What Pete did was up to him and out of their hands.

He now needed to focus on Amy and figure out if the two of them had a future. Del knew what he wanted. After dinner at Thorn's, he'd take her back to the cabin for a long talk.

Glancing up, he saw Bobby, his youngest deputy, standing in the doorway.

"You've got a call from Mayor Barnes, Sheriff."

"Thanks, Bobby." He picked up the phone. "Good afternoon, Mayor. What can I do for you?"

"I heard a rumor, Del, and I called to see if it's accurate."

Del pinched the bridge of his nose, not eager to discuss hearsay with the mayor.

"It's about you, Del."

He straightened, holding the phone in a tight grip. "What's the rumor?"

"I hear you've been seen around town with Amy Peterson. Isn't she Pete Peterson's daughter?"

His jaw hardened. "Yes, she is."

"You know, some folks might not like to have the sheriff befriending the daughter of a felon. A man who's a known criminal, who is still most likely involved in illegal activities. It would be a shame for a friendship with her to play a part in the next election for sheriff."

Gritting his teeth, Del sucked in a slow breath, letting it out before answering. "My private life is my own, Mayor."

"Not when it involves one of the Petersons."

"Amy has nothing to do with her father's activities. She and her mother moved away years ago and Amy hasn't seen him since."

"That may be, Del. Remember, people have long memories. I wouldn't advise you getting too close to the Peterson woman or you might find yourself having to make a choice."

"Choice?"

"The woman or the job. Like I said, lots of things get thrown out during an election. I wouldn't want your choice to affect whether or not you continue as sheriff."

Del and the mayor had often butted heads, disagreeing on many things since they'd both been elected. He also knew the man had backed the other candidate when Del ran for sheriff.

"I appreciate your concern, Mayor. I'll take it under advisement."

"You do that, Del. Now, I best get going."

Hanging up, Del mumbled a curse. It was one more jab from a man who played politics well, grabbing power whenever he saw an opportunity. Del wasn't going to change his plans or let Amy go, refusing to let the mayor's comments bother him. He had more faith in the people of Whiskey Bend.

"Sorry, Sheriff. You've got another call. Kull Kacey is on hold for you."

Del shook off his anger as he grabbed the phone. "I expected you to call my cell, Kull."

"I tried, but it went to voicemail."

Del grimaced. He'd turned off his phone when he had lunch with Amy. "Did you talk with Pete?"

"Yep. As you'd expect, he didn't take it well. I've only seen him this mad one other time, and that's when Vivian refused to talk to him after moving out."

Rubbing the back of his neck, Del felt a stab of dread. "What do you think he's going to do?"

"I don't know and I didn't ask. Best thing we can do is put it behind us. We're heading back to Whiskey Bend tomorrow morning. Come by for a beer tomorrow night, and bring Amy."

"Will do, Kull."

Hanging up, he wondered how long it would take for Pete to make a move. If his suspicions were correct, he didn't think it would take long at all.

Chapter Fifteen

Dinner was a celebration of Amy's new job, as well as a night Boone introduced Jenny and Tyler to Grace and Thorn. They welcomed them without a hint of surprise.

Amy and Jenny remembered each other from high school, falling into an easy discussion of their lives while Thorn, Boone, and Del took Tyler outside to play catch. When Grace called them in for dinner, Thorn placed an arm across Boone's shoulders.

"I'll be at the ranch tomorrow to help and I expect all the details."

Boone drew in a breath, nodding. "There's a lot I have to tell you." He looked at Del. "You planning to be out tomorrow?"

Del let the door close behind him. "Wouldn't miss it."

"This looks great." Thorn glanced at the table filled with meat, pasta, salad, and bread. "When did you have time to cook all this?" Wrapping an arm around Grace's waist, he pulled her close, kissing her cheek.

"Finished my assignments last night. That left me all of today."

Amy watched the way they gazed at each other. No one could mistake the love between them. Glancing at Del, she saw him watching her, wondering what he was thinking. She didn't have to wait long. Pulling out her chair, he let her sit down before bending over to whisper in her ear.

"I love you."

Looking up, she mouthed the same.

Thorn chuckled. "Okay, you two. I know Del's been gone a few days, but try to keep your hands to yourselves until after dinner."

For the second time that day, Del wanted to flip his brother off. Instead, he smiled, leaning down to kiss Amy again as Grace began passing around the food.

"Take as much as you want. I've got more in the kitchen." Grace looked at Tyler as he heaped pasta onto his plate. "How old are you, Tyler?"

He held up his hand, showing four fingers and a thumb. "Five."

Amy glanced at Jenny. "Is he in school yet?"

Nodding, her eyes clouded. "Kindergarten. You'll be in first grade next year, right, buddy?"

"Uh-huh."

Grace swallowed her food, rinsing it down with water. "Where do you two live, Jenny?"

"Outside of town in the house where I grew up. My parents died several years ago and left it to me. Boone has been over several times, building a ramp, modifying a few doors so I can get through them with my chair." She glanced at him, her gratitude clear in the way her eyes held his.

"Uncle Boone is teaching me how to ride."

"Is that right?" Thorn asked, glancing at Boone.

"Uh-huh. So I can ride when I live with him." Tyler shoveled another spoonful of food into his mouth, oblivious to the expressions around the table.

Thorn's eyes narrowed on Boone. "Moving in with you?"

Jenny licked her lips, clearing her throat, taking a quick look at Tyler, who seemed absorbed in his meal. "I'll let Boone explain the specifics." She swallowed, sucking in a shaky breath. "In a few weeks, Ty will need a new home. Boone has decided to adopt him."

The room fell into silence as Thorn, Grace, and Amy let her meaning sink in. Reaching toward Del, Amy grabbed his hand, gripping it tightly.

"Yep. It will be our man cave. Right, Ty?"

"With horses?"

Boone glanced over Tyler's head at Jenny. "Yeah, buddy. With horses. And all these people will be part of your family." His throat tightened, knowing Jenny had little time left to enjoy Tyler. The thought broke his heart.

Grace forced a grim smile. "When Uncle Boone is too busy, I'll be happy to ride with you, Ty."

Amy nodded. "Me, too, Ty. Grace is teaching me to ride and I love it."

"Uncle Boone says I can have my own horse when I get grown enough to take care of it."

Boone ruffled Tyler's hair. "The way you're growing, it won't be long." He pushed aside his own fear, as well as the doubt he held at becoming the boy's adoptive father.

Standing, Grace began picking up empty plates. "Hope you all left room for dessert."

Del and Amy drove back to the cabin in silence, holding hands, each grappling with the reality Jenny had a short time left with her son. Amy fought to keep her tears under control as they walked inside, turning on lights.

She latched onto Del's hand again. "You already knew."

"Boone told me last Sunday when I showed up at the ranch. Jenny and Ty were already there. He stopped by my place later that night after he'd taken them home." Setting his hat on a hook, he ran a hand through his hair. "The papers are already signed, everything's in place so there won't be any issues when Jenny...when she's gone."

Amy sat down on the sofa, pulling him down next to her. "How much time does she have?"

"A few weeks at most. Before we left, Boone told me it could be as soon as a week."

"I can't imagine." Amy placed a hand over her mouth to stifle a sob. It all seemed so unfair.

"Boone will make a good father."

Her eyes softened. "He'll make an *excellent* father. And you and Thorn will make terrific uncles."

Del stroked a hand down her hair. "And you and Grace will be amazing aunts."

Amy stilled, her breath hitching. "Me?"

Turning to face her, Del took her hands in his. "I know we've had a quick and somewhat rough start."

She shook her head. "Not a traditional relationship."

A grim smile crossed his face. "No, not traditional. It doesn't mean we can't start fresh, make it right."

Amy's heart began to beat so fast, she thought he might hear it. "What are you saying?"

"I know we've got a ways to go, but I love you, Amy. What I'm asking is for us to begin again, get to know each other in a way we haven't been able to do since you returned to Whiskey Bend."

"Date?"

He chuckled, his fingers brushing down her cheek. "Dating would be part of it."

She sucked in a breath at his touch. "Spending time with your family?"

"That would be another part." Moving his hand to the back of her neck, he drew her toward him. "This would be another part." Lowering his head, he skimmed the briefest of kisses across her lips.

"I like that part." She moved her hands up his arms to his shoulders, wrapping them around his neck to pull him back down.

"Hmmm...I like that part, too."

She glanced up at him, her eyes sparkling with mischief. "Do we have to wait for all the other *parts* before we..." Amy drew his bottom lip into her mouth, hearing him groan.

In a quick move, he lifted her, settling her on his lap. "I think that horse ran out of the barn a week ago, darlin'."

"I'm thinking the same thing."

Standing, he held her close to his chest as he walked down the hall to his bedroom. "Good. That's one thing we can agree on."

Everyone showed up at the ranch the following day. Grace had volunteered to pick up Jenny, Tyler, and Amy, suggesting they stop in town for groceries. It had been both a good and bad idea as Tyler wandered with them through the aisles, finding one snack after another.

Jenny allowed him two, pulling out cash when they reached the cashier.

"Put away your money. This is on Thorn and me."

Jenny shook her head. "I can't let you do that after having us over for dinner last night."

Placing a hand on her arm, Grace smiled. "Let us do this."

Amy watched the exchange, her heart squeezing. After last night, she knew without a doubt she and Del would make it. They'd talked of having children, how many, and where they'd live. Amy told Del she planned to keep working as long as she could.

Watching Jenny and Tyler at the ranch, knowing how much the young woman would miss, Amy now wondered if staying home with her and Del's children, at least until the last entered school, might be workable. It was something they'd talk about when the time was right.

Grace gave Tyler and Amy another riding lesson as Jenny watched from under the shade of an old tree. Afterward, they fixed lunch, everyone sitting around the large table discussing ranch business, Thorn's shop, and Del's trip to Idaho, careful not to say too much with Tyler listening to every word.

"So it wasn't Pete?" Boone grabbed a handful of chips from a bowl, popping one into his mouth.

"Not from what we learned. Kull rode out to White Basin to let Pete know."

Thorn switched his gaze from Grace to Del. "What do you think he'll do?"

Del shook his head. "Honestly, I don't know."

"And you probably don't care. I know I wouldn't." Boone took a long swallow of his water.

Shrugging, Del refused to be drawn into a discussion of what might happen to Bear. His gut told him the man wouldn't last long.

"Do you plan to visit your father, Amy?"

Setting down her sandwich, she seemed to mull it over. "It's something I've been thinking about."

Reaching under the table, Del took hold of her hand. "Let me know when and we'll go together."

"You'd want to meet him?"

Del lifted a brow. "He's your father. Of course I want to meet him."

She tilted her head to one side. "He's also an ex-felon."

"I figure if he can get over me being a lawman, I can get over him being an outlaw."

Boone laughed at the exchange. "Hey, I think we should all go up and meet him. Wonder if he'd want to come to one of our Sunday dinners."

Amy tilted back her head and laughed. "I couldn't say, but would sure like to see his face when you invite him."

The week passed in a blur, Amy and Del driving into town together each morning and returning to the cabin together each night. Neither mentioned the sleeping arrangements, coming to an unspoken understanding they'd be in the same bed.

He'd taken her to dinner twice, once at a restaurant on the way to Missoula and once at Doc's Grill and Tavern. Saturday, they'd be back at the ranch with plans to take a long drive into the mountains on Sunday.

Friday evening, Del pulled to a stop in front of Gray Wolf, waiting for Amy, when the unmistakable sound of a siren caught his attention. A minute later, an emergency paramedic vehicle flew past, heading out of town. Seeing Amy exit the building, he motioned her to hurry to the car, then took off.

"What is it?" Reaching to her side, she pulled out the seat belt, clicking it closed.

"An ambulance is heading out of town." He flipped on his siren, then gripped the wheel.

Seeing his intense expression, Amy stilled. "Do you think it's Jenny?"

"I don't know, but if it is, I want to be at the house with Tyler until Boone arrives."

Nodding, she said a silent prayer for Jenny and her son. As they followed the paramedics, taking one turn, then another, it became clear it was heading in the direction of Jenny's house.

"Please, no," Amy whispered as Del pulled to a stop behind the ambulance.

"Wait here." Jumping out, Del ran to the door, following the paramedics inside. Several minutes later, he reappeared, carrying a screaming Tyler in his arms.

Amy left the car and ran to them, taking Tyler from Del. "It will be all right, sweetheart." She smoothed a hand over his hair, talking in a soft whisper, doing her best to lessen his pain while Del called Boone, then Thorn.

"They're both on their way." His focus returned to the house when the paramedics came outside, walking alongside a gurney, Jenny's head covered with a blanket.

Amy did her best to keep Tyler with her, but one glance at the paramedics and he pulled free, racing toward his mother. He didn't get far before Del's strong arms wrapped around his waist, holding him to his chest.

"She's at peace now, Ty." Feeling his own tears threatening, Del willed them away as his throat tightened. Turning away, he saw Amy leaning against his car, tears streaming down her face.

He didn't know how long they stood there, watching the paramedics load the gurney, before one of them came over to speak with Del. Handing Tyler to Amy, he and the man moved several feet away.

"I'm sorry, Sheriff. She didn't make it."

Del nodded.

"She was on a list we're given for people with terminal illnesses. We'd been expecting the call."

Once more, Del nodded. "Thank you. We knew Jenny didn't have much time."

The squealing of tires had them both turning. Boone jumped out of his truck, rushing to the ambulance.

"I need to see her."

"I'm sorry, sir, but—"

"It's all right. Let Mr. Macklin take a quick look. He's listed as family on our report."

Boone looked at the paramedic standing next to him, recognizing him from high school. "Thank you."

Climbing inside, he watched as the paramedic lifted the blanket. His features softened as he bent down, stroking his fingers down her cheek, then kissed her forehead. "I promise, Jenny. Ty will be well loved. He'll grow up the way you wanted, in a family who'll teach him how to grow into a man you'd be proud of." Stroking her cheek once more, he placed a soft kiss on her lips. "I'll never let him forget you."

Standing, Boone's knees buckled as he stepped out of the ambulance. Del's arm circled his waist, keeping him standing.

"Where's Ty?"

Del nodded toward Amy. "Right there, waiting for you."

By the time they loaded Tyler's clothes and toys into Boone's old truck and returned to the ranch, it was past dinnertime. Grace arrived with two large pizzas, although no one, including Tyler, seemed too interested.

After Boone settled Tyler in bed, they all said their goodbyes, planning to meet back at the ranch the next morning.

Once they reached the cabin, Del walked around the car, opening Amy's door. Holding out his hand, he helped her out, wrapping an arm around her shoulders as they went inside.

"How about a glass of wine?" Del asked, walking into the kitchen.

"Wine would be great."

They settled onto the sofa, neither speaking as they sipped their wine. After a while, Del stood, put his glass down, and headed to the bedroom. A minute later, he returned, kneeling in front of Amy, taking her hand.

Her lips parted at the intense, yet vulnerable expression on his face.

"I know we agreed to take our time, make sure we were both certain about us. The thing is, I'm already certain. I love you, Amy. I've never said those words to another woman, and never will. Marry me, sweetheart. Be my wife."

She didn't know if it was the strain of the past few hours or shock, but new tears appeared, along with a brilliant smile. Nodding, she lunged forward, wrapping her arms around his neck.

"I love you, Del. Yes, I'll marry you."

Epilogue

One week later...

Jenny's graveside service took place on a clear, warm Friday before a crowd of over fifty people. Friends from school, co-workers, and townsfolk who'd watched her grow up stood in silent remembrance of a vibrant young woman who'd been taken from them much too soon.

Boone held Tyler's small hand, feeling the young boy shake. Without saying a word, Boone leaned down, lifting him into his arms. Thorn and Grace stood on one side of them, Del and Amy on the other. He'd never been more grateful for the support of his family. His throat tightened at the acute feeling of loss. He'd loved her as a friend, as a good mother, a woman who fought hard, even during the worst of times. Boone would never forget her, and he'd make certain Tyler didn't, either.

As the minister spoke the final prayer, Boone's gaze wandered over the crowd. She'd talked of friends, people she cared about in Whiskey Bend, and they all came out to honor her life today. His back stiffened when he saw Willow Robinson across from him, standing with her parents. Her eyes met his for a brief moment before she shifted toward Jenny's coffin, lowering her gaze. For an instant, Boone saw an intense look of despair on her face, mirroring his own misery. He'd made so many mistakes, Willow being the biggest. If only...

"We'll drive you back to the ranch." Thorn's voice shook him out of the depressing path his thoughts had taken.

Nodding, he set Tyler on the ground, grabbing his hand. "Do you want to say goodbye to Mommy one more time?"

Tyler's big, round eyes looked up at Boone, his lower lip trembling.

"Come on, buddy. We'll do it together." Pulling two flowers from a large bouquet, he handed one to Tyler, then turned, his features strained. "We love you, Jenny, and we'll never forget you." Boone placed the flower on the casket, nodding for Tyler to do the same.

"I love you, Mommy." His small hand shook as he laid the flower next to Boone's, then looked up. "Is she happy now, Uncle Boone?"

His throat clogged as he worked to control his own tears. "Yes. Mommy is happy now." Glancing up, he once again saw Willow looking at him, her soft blue eyes moving between him and Tyler before she turned away to join her parents.

"Are you ready?" Del's whispered words had Boone taking one last look at the casket before following his family to their trucks.

Del and Amy had picked him and Tyler up. They rode back with Thorn and Grace. He knew many of the people at the memorial service would be at the ranch, bringing food, wanting a chance to see Tyler. Most would be curious to see how Boone, a man they knew to be a staunch bachelor, would handle parenthood. The answer evaded him, but he refused to dwell on that now.

Once they pulled to a stop, Boone lifted Tyler out of the truck. "How about we go check the horses?"

The boy's face lit with excitement. Before Boone could say another word, he started running toward the barn.

Grace walked up next to him. "Thorn and I will go with him. You head inside and see to the guests."

Del approached from his other side, Amy's hand in one of his, the other clasping Boone on the back. "Come on, little brother. Let's get this over with."

Boone nodded at Del. "What I really want is a whiskey. Maybe two."

"We're all right with you."

Inside, people were already mingling, plates of food in their hands as they spoke about Jenny, Tyler, and Boone becoming the boy's guardian.

"You're going to do just fine, kiddo." Kull stood beside him, holding out a shot of whiskey. "Take it. No one will fault you one bit. And don't ever think Jenny didn't go in peace. You made her leaving bearable, and I'm mighty proud of you for that."

A grateful expression passed over Boone's face as he took the glass, tossing back the amber liquid. He had no idea what the next weeks, months, and years would bring. All he could do was his best and hope, as Jenny looked down on them, she'd be happy with what she saw.

The following day, Del and Amy arrived at the ranch for their normal Saturday routine, Kull in the back seat. Thorn and Grace pulled in a few minutes later. There'd be no need to cook today. Friends and neighbors had left enough food to last for weeks.

Joining them as they walked up the steps, Boone held the door open for Tyler, who jumped into Del's arms.

"Aunt Grace is teaching me to ride again today, Uncle Del."

He swung Tyler around, marveling at the way young kids could cope with even the worst of losses. "I think Amy may want to join you. If you two do real good, you can ride out to the pasture where we'll be working."

Tyler raised a fist into the air. "Yes!"

Chuckling, Del set him down, nodding toward Grace and Amy. "You go ahead. We'll check on how you're doing before we ride out."

Thorn, Boone, and Kull walked up to join him as Tyler ran to the barn.

Boone crossed his arms, shaking his head. "Why do my instincts tell me a day with Ty is going to wear me out much more than a day working the ranch?"

The three looked at him, shrugging.

"Great. I'm going to be doing this with the help of men who've never had children. God help me." Boone chuckled, then slapped Del on the back. "I just wanted to say congratulations again. My head hasn't been right the last week, but I'm happy for you and Amy."

Del pulled him into a quick embrace. "Thanks. I don't have a clue what I'm getting into, but at least I have Thorn to help me."

Thorn chuckled. "Don't take your cues from me. I'm still a beginner when it comes to married life. You two figure out a date yet?"

Shaking his head, Del watched as Grace brought Tyler's horse outside, followed by Amy leading Sunshine. "Haven't had time to talk about it. Amy wants to visit Pete in White Basin to tell him about us getting married first. If we can both get away, we're looking at next month to head over."

"Before you boys saddle your horses, you need to know about a call I got this week. With Jenny's service, I didn't want to say anything sooner."

"Who'd you speak with, Kull?" Del asked.

"Not going to say, but the message was, *Vivian got her justice.*"

Del's brows lifted, his gaze darting to where Amy stood next to Grace and Tyler. "So it's over?"

Kull nodded. "I don't know any more than what I just said, but I'd say yes. It's up to you to tell Amy. She might want to know before you make your road trip." Slipping his hands into his pockets, Kull pierced Del with a hard look. "One more thing, Sheriff."

Del's eyes widened. "What's that?"

"You ever make my baby girl cry, you'll answer to me."

"And me," Thorn chimed in.

"Appears you'll be dealing with all of us, big brother." Boone smiled for the first time in a week.

Looking at his brothers and a man who'd become like a father to them, Del threw back his head and laughed. "Guess the pressure's on."

Can a second chance at love rescue two people from a shared tragic past? Start reading Boone's story to find out!

If you want to keep current on all my preorders, new releases, and other happenings, sign up for my newsletter at: http://www.shirleendavies.com/contact-me.html

A Note from Shirleen

Thank you for taking the time to read **Del**!

If you enjoyed it, please consider telling your friends or posting a short review. Word of mouth is an author's best friend and much appreciated.

I care about quality, so if you find something in error, please contact me via email at shirleen@shirleendavies.com

Books by Shirleen Davies

Contemporary Western Romance Series

MacLarens of Fire Mountain

Second Summer, Book One
Hard Landing, Book Two
One More Day, Book Three
All Your Nights, Book Four
Always Love You, Book Five
Hearts Don't Lie, Book Six
No Getting Over You, Book Seven
'Til the Sun Comes Up, Book Eight
Foolish Heart, Book Nine

Macklins of Whiskey Bend

Thorn, Book One
Del, Book Two
Boone, Book Three

Historical Western Romance Series
Redemption Mountain

Redemption's Edge, Book One
Wildfire Creek, Book Two
Sunrise Ridge, Book Three

Dixie Moon, Book Four
Survivor Pass, Book Five
Promise Trail, Book Six
Deep River, Book Seven
Courage Canyon, Book Eight
Forsaken Falls, Book Nine
Solitude Gorge, Book Ten
Rogue Rapids, Book Eleven
Angel Peak, Book Twelve
Restless Wind, Book Thirteen
Storm Summit, Book Fourteen
Mystery Mesa, Book Fifteen
Thunder Valley, Book Sixteen
A Very Splendor Christmas, Holiday Novella, Book Seventeen
Paradise Point, Book Eighteen,
Silent Sunset, Book Nineteen
Rocky Basin, Book Twenty, Coming Next in the Series!

MacLarens of Fire Mountain

Tougher than the Rest, Book One
Faster than the Rest, Book Two
Harder than the Rest, Book Three
Stronger than the Rest, Book Four
Deadlier than the Rest, Book Five
Wilder than the Rest, Book Six

MacLarens of Boundary Mountain

Colin's Quest, Book One,
Brodie's Gamble, Book Two
Quinn's Honor, Book Three
Sam's Legacy, Book Four
Heather's Choice, Book Five
Nate's Destiny, Book Six
Blaine's Wager, Book Seven
Fletcher's Pride, Book Eight
Bay's Desire, Book Nine
Cam's Hope, Book Ten

Romantic Suspense

Eternal Brethren, Military Romantic Suspense

Steadfast, Book One
Shattered, Book Two
Haunted, Book Three
Untamed, Book Four
Devoted, Book Five
Faithful, Book Six
Exposed, Book Seven
Undaunted, Book Eight
Resolute, Book Nine
Unspoken, Book Ten
Defiant, Book Eleven
Consumed, Book Twelve, Coming Next in the Series!

Peregrine Bay, Romantic Suspense

Reclaiming Love, Book One
Our Kind of Love, Book Two
Edge of Love, Book Three, Coming Next in the Series!

Find all of my books at:
https://www.shirleendavies.com/books.html

About the Shirleen

Shirleen Davies writes romance—historical, contemporary, and romantic suspense. She grew up in Southern California, attended Oregon State University, and has degrees from San Diego State University and the University of Maryland. During the day she provides consulting services to small and mid-sized businesses. But her real passion is writing emotionally charged stories of flawed people who find redemption through love and acceptance. She now lives with her husband in a beautiful town in northern Arizona.

I love to hear from my readers!

Send me an email: shirleen@shirleendavies.com
Visit my Website: https://www.shirleendavies.com/
Sign up to be notified of New Releases:
https://www.shirleendavies.com/contact/
Follow me on Amazon:
http://www.amazon.com/author/shirleendavies
Follow me on BookBub:
https://www.bookbub.com/authors/shirleen-davies

Other ways to connect with me:

Facebook Author Page:
http://www.facebook.com/shirleendaviesauthor
Pinterest: http://pinterest.com/shirleendavies

Instagram:
https://www.instagram.com/shirleendavies_author/
TikTok: shirleendavies_author
Twitter: www.twitter.com/shirleendavies

Avalanche Ranch Press, LLC
PO Box 12618
Prescott, AZ 86304